London Love

By
VICTORIA ATKIN

London Love by Victoria Atkin
Published by Evatopia Press
http://www.evatopia.com
8447 Wilshire Blvd., Ste. 401, Beverly Hills, CA 90211
a division of Evatopia, Inc.

Two Actors.

One Ambition.

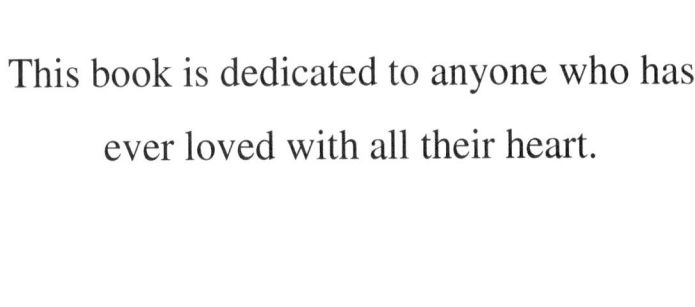

This book is dedicated to anyone who has ever loved with all their heart.

Prologue

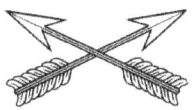

Leaning out an upstairs window of a comfortable sized brick house on the East coast of Southern England near London, a handsome man beamed down at the arrival of a shiny black Volkswagen Golf that pulled up at the front of his house.

A familiar young woman turned off the car engine and stepped out of the vehicle, whilst the man at the window hurried to finish brushing his teeth. Excited by her arrival, his cheeky and youthful grin grew with an overwhelming happiness upon seeing her once more.

Like many actors, the man was strikingly handsome standing over six-foot-tall, cleanly shaven with piercing, blue eyes. Those eyes matched his bright sapphire blue t-shirt, strategically V-necked to display his mouthwatering collarbone and sculpted upper chest, which concealed his thumping heart.

Opening the front door, he paused while taking in the young woman who stood before him. His smile broadened before kissing her indulgently without speaking a word.

She dropped her small suitcase in the hallway without ceremony, wasting no time to fall into his arms. She lifted his top upwards as his heartbreaking, dark brown, head of hair emerged through. Her loving smile prevailed as he tossed his shirt to the floor.

# # #

Chapter 1

Five Years Earlier...

Summer was drawing to a close and the crisp air coated the cobblestones of the West End's Theatreland with a light frost as dawn broke. The city of London was predominately the country's central hub for all things actor related. In the heart of it all was Shaftesbury Avenue where the grand theatres stood proudly on either side of the historical street.

London was just waking up, calm and peaceful. The timelessness of the town was undeterred by the tourists that would soon pound its wise pavements. Its magic captured the attention of the world and professional cameras complete with Neoprene neck straps would soon snap at articles of interest.

At the top of the street stood the Palace Theatre. Broad in size and by far the greediest in the surface area it spanned, this grand theatre was cemented firmly in its own pride. An understandably boastful building with its royal red bricks renouncing a lifetime of dedication to

British theatre. Tonight, the string of white lights would be once again switched on, fringing the entrance as excited theatre lovers would enjoy a night entertained by thespians.

A little further down the infamous avenue was The Queens Theatre, who continued to house the longstanding musical show Les Miserables, "for over 25 years," the front billboard described. Next to the front entrance of the Queens Theatre was a bar and adjacent to that, another theatre, The Gielgud, named after the late John Gielgud, a warm man and a well loved British figure who had generously dedicated his life to the art of all things acting. The bar that sat in between the seasoned theatre venues was hip and trendy having recently enjoyed a well needed revamp.

The golden, summer sun rose and so began the chilly morning stirring of the eight million and three hundred thousand people that resided in the populous city, testing the lowering climate with the tips of their toes as they contemplated emerging from the warmth of their heavy duvets. A crisp, fresh air blew through the windows of those who left them ajar to perfectly counterbalance the central heating.

Under the city another world awoke. The transport for the London tube system covered 249 miles underneath the capital. Nineteen thousands workers dressed to serve the London underground system that day as the tunnel walls prepared to be shaken once more from the rattling of the trains that escorted thousands.

A Bakerloo line tube ride away from Shaftesbury Avenue, changing at Baker street to catch the Metropolitan line was Finchley Road tube station.

Located in a north westerly direction of central London and bustling as usual, the shouts from the traditional fruit and vegetable stand announcing "two for a pound" on fresh red Cox's apples, depicted the daily scene.

Commuters rushed towards the departing trains in sharp, dry-cleaned tailored suits, carrying fold away bikes and backpacks, the bleeps of Oyster cards tapping as barriers opened under the command of the electronic instruction claiming the appropriate credit for the journey ahead.

A five-minute walk turning left out of the station passing the Walkabout and WetherSpoons public houses was home to three young twenty-something-year-old professionals. Trying professionals more accurately described, they worked hard but mainly got drunk and attempted to survive on diets of cereal and chicken breasts, but never at the same time because they did have some standards. A few months earlier they had moved to the Finchley Road area of West London after one of them had rounded the others up, convincing them to move out of their country comforts and bite the big city bullet.

In this apartment lived Evelyn Wise.

# # #

Chapter 2

There was no banister on the staircase and the carpet had been hauled up by the owner in a rage, ripping through the house like a blazing fire. It was a masculine home complete with a full size pool table. In a word: minimalistic.

At the front of the house lived a selection of cars, projects awaiting attention. A fort of a silent warrior. Jack King awoke to the sound of his trusty radio. His strong, stubbled jaw rolled from the squashed pillow as he searched the floor for some gym clothes. The voice of the cheerful BBC Radio 2 host accompanied him in his morning ritual.

Beside him lay a brown short and stout Pit Bull, which snored contentedly. Other than his trusty companion, he lived alone and had done so for several years, convincing himself it was easier that way. The time was used to heal a wounded heart.

# # #

The Finchley Road trio had fun in their humble abode, their first steps in the big city unfamiliar and rather daunting in comparison to their countryside upbringings. The change of scenery was exciting and any fears they had were easily fixed with a trip to the fruit machine in the pub or a Karaoke night at Walkabout.

Evelyn Wise had worked at The Queens Theatre for few weeks to fund the final part of her education, the general thought being she might make some useful contacts, that was, if by chance, a huge director were to walk into the most watched theatre show on earth and be interested in the only English girl behind the bar.

The pay was poor, but her enticing feminine charms often excused her from really getting her hands dirty, unconsciously delegating the work to the male admirers willing to do it for her. It wasn't that she was afraid of hard work, but a bar job was by no means satisfactory for a girl like Evelyn. It was simply a means to an end.

# # #

Parking his parents' compact borrowed car in Holborn, a bubble car too small for a man like Jack King, he illegally displayed a handy disabled badge and cooly clambered out. Jack enjoyed his early evening strolls to the Gielgud Theatre, savoring the taste of his romantic home city and the streets he had grown up discovering, which he now knew like the back of his hand.

He walked with a spring in his step, finally part of a real cast on a proper West End stage complete with his own dressing room. He wasn't the lead, but he polished his part to perfection and would make sure everyone knew who he was.

It was a Thursday in May and the bar at The Queens theatre was busy that night. The summer holidays were about to take off and although a great number of the theatres in London went dark over the summer, Les Miserables continued its run by popular demand.

For every performance a member of staff was chosen to stand outside the bar and take interval orders by hand. Most people didn't mind this; they even got tips, but Evelyn dreaded being picked. She turned to making carefully planned excuses, which eventually allowed one of her work admirers to step in and save the day. It wasn't talking to the customers that bothered her, but the mathematical pursuit of doing all the sums in her head that left her nervous. Numbers scared her, adding up and giving change even more. She hadn't listened in maths class, preferring to sing for her sums, aggravating her young teacher in the process.

But today, there was no getting out of it. The patrons arrived and the queue for interval orders began. Her black biro pen doodled on the notepad. A handsomely dressed man ordered champagne for him and his new fiancée's engagement, making Evelyn think of her own boyfriend fleetingly before returning her mind to the job at hand. She did love him in her own way, but it had been evident for a long time that he wasn't right for her.

A group of mid-thirty-year-old men gathered by the Gielgud theatre stage door as Evelyn changed out of her uniform. She removed her theatre waistcoat in the maroon colored paint peeling public toilet cubicle inside the Queens Theatre, whilst the orchestra began to strike up for the second act. It wasn't the easiest of changes, in some respect mimicking the changes the actors endured in the small, dark spaces backstage.

Tonight, Evelyn would leap into the breach as the show next door housed a play starring an actress she loved and would close after its short six week run the following week. She would wait for a chance to speak with her on her exit. The only other thing she had waiting at home was an empty fridge and missed calls from a boyfriend she had perhaps fallen out of love with. A relationship that should have finished six months after it had begun.

The comfort and social pressure to be "in a relationship" even before Facebook offered the option, had relieved an anxiety from the rest of her life struggles and so she was labelled his girlfriend of three years.

As Evelyn exited the stage door of the Queens Theatre, the evening was still light and the summer air was warm from the enjoyable, slightly muggy heat. She smiled.

Scuffing her small feet, wondering how long she might have to wait, she happily walked left out of the stage door exit, relieved she had finished her shift. A sense of optimism began to set in as the opportunity to meet a heroine of hers began to dawn. She often had these somewhat random ideas, a burning excitement to break through the unconscious society rule book and test foreign waters.

Plugging her headphones in, pressing play on her iPod Nano, she leant against the wall of the adjacent theatre from where she worked, alleviating her aching feet from standing behind the bar and watched as the same group of thirty something year old men laughed with one and other.

Eventually, the group embraced the opportunity to strike up a conversation with Evelyn.

"So what brings you here?" the tallest man questioned exaggerating the cheesy chat up line teasingly. They were real Londoners.

"Well...I'm waiting for Juliet Carpenter. I've just graduated from drama school as an actress and I would love to meet her," Evelyn proclaimed enthusiastically with an innocence the men were intrigued by.

"Juliet Carpenter is my mum," the leader of the pack called over.

"Yer, I am sure she is!" Evelyn replied.

"Honestly, if you don't believe me, come up with us and say hello."

Unaware of Evelyn's fearlessness, the man was half surprised when she cooly replied, "Okay. I would love to say hello to your mum."

# # #

Chapter 3

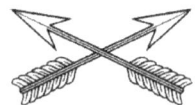

Inside the theatre, the play had just finished, the actors retiring to their dressing rooms after a rapturous applause and their traditional finale bows before the curtains were drawn after another successful performance.

Checking his mobile phone, Jack King replied to a text message and headed down the old spiral staircase, his hand placed firmly on the historic wooden bannister, leaving his dressing room to the Gielgud stage door. Reaching the bottom of the stairs, he pushed through a black door and gave permission to his audience members waiting outside to be allowed up to his dressing room.

This was not theatre protocol, but he had managed to execute the mission quickly as not to draw attention to it. Cheekily poking his head around the door, he quickly addressed one of his friends, not yet greeting the rest of the group. That would happen once they were through stage door security.

As the men piled into his dressing room, Jack noticed they were joined by an attractive, young girl, someone he had not met before and made the assumption she must be an unofficial girlfriend to one of them. And yet, from his memory, they were all already attached.

# # #

Evelyn surveyed her new surroundings excited by the prospect of meeting an acting idol. As she searched the dressing room it slowly dawned on her that she was the only female and that Juliet Carpenter was no where to be seen. The heavy wooden dressing room door slammed forcefully shut behind her.

Jack introduced his friends one by one. Included was a shorter guy at the end of the room, who hadn't been part of the crowd outside and was a new face to all of them except Jack. Paler than Jack and fairly timid in comparison, John Wild, another actor from the show, smiled pleasantly. Photos of his smiling friends and family were wedged between the mirror and its frame. A fiction book lay beside a script and a palette of theatre makeup rested on the ledge immediately in front of him.

John was polite looking, a young man with wispy, bright orange hair who carried himself with a boyish innocence. Jack completed his introductions looking towards the nameless and unfamiliar girl.

Jack was thirty-six, six-foot-one with dark shiny hair, its perfect length and thickness like a man from a shampoo advert. During the show he had dyed it with a home hair kit, a Loreal packet he had purchased from the pharmacy store Boots, that added a hint of red to his dark locks in his attempt to pick up the theatre lighting and disguise the grey.

Smiling, he approached her. "Hi, I'm Jack King." His eyes fixed on the curious young woman.

"Evelyn Wise" she replied, slightly dismissively, but introducing herself nonetheless.

"So how do you know this lot?"

"I met them outside," she smiled coyly.

Jack laughed, unsure if she were joking or telling the truth. "You mean, you don't know each other?" Jack was puzzled by who this mysterious woman was. Surely she hadn't just wandered in with his friends. They must have known her.

"Nope. Apparently Juliet Carpenter is his mum," she joked, looking towards the man who had expressed this white lie outside.

"There she is...my mum!" The guy pointed towards Jack who, by now, was entirely confused, but entertained by it all.

"Would you like to join us for a glass of red wine? It's not the cheap stuff," Jack offered politely.

Evelyn had a taste for alcohol and thought while she waited to find Juliet this may quench that desire. Jack offered her a seat, which Evelyn declined, not wanting to stay too long. She would stick to her primary objective and meet Juliet; she had gotten this far.

# # #

Evelyn Wise was twenty-three, petite and tom boyish in her demeanor. Her eyes captivatingly brown against her long blonde hair, which was tied back from her face -- the only evidence of her recent bar shift.

Uninterested in her immediate environment, she impatiently asked Jack, "So, do you know Juliet? Seeings as it is not his mum, maybe you can introduce me?"

Although she never thought of herself as cute, Jack smiled and laughed off the question, aggravating Evelyn who wanted to be taken seriously. Who was this arrogant, although slightly good-looking older man?

As the wine flowed, Evelyn's impatience to meet Juliet had subsided and she caught herself falling somewhat for Jack's charms. Unconsciously the room became divided as Jack and Evelyn realised they had a great deal in common. The mission to find Juliet diminishing from her thoughts as she connected with Jack unexpectedly.

The night grew later and the other dressing rooms back stage began to empty. Jack remained curious about Evelyn. He silenced his thoughts, which were becoming excited by this chance encounter. Jack had fallen for her almost immediately, but Evelyn had not yet acknowledged the impact this meeting would have.

# # #

Chapter 4

A missed call reported on the screen of her mobile phone. It listed her boyfriend's long distance number as she retrieved it from her bag to check the time. Jack seized the opportunity to casually ask her for her number. Although she had had a great evening it wasn't something she was interested in pursuing further. His phone was placed in her hands as she discussed these thoughts with herself.

Really, giving an older man she had only just met her number when she was in a relationship -- a solid one at that, even if it was rather dull. She chided herself that the topic of her boyfriend hadn't arisen in her conversations with Jack, which mainly revolved around their shared passion of acting. He would just have to end up as someone she would have to politely avoid texting back until he realised she wasn't interested.

Finally, she took hold of this virtual stranger's phone, pressing the keys as she entered a mobile number into a cheap pay as you go handset. Unbeknownst to the Jack, the final digit was entered incorrectly. She knew it was a cheap trick, but didn't have the courage to politely tell him she would rather they never spoke again.

Warmed by the alcohol, the group joyfully made their way down the old theatre staircase as Jack confidently flirted with Evelyn, slapping her on the bottom, which Evelyn found entirely inappropriate and became quickly disappointed and repelled, now looking forward to the tube ride home.

As they said goodbye outside the theatre stage door exit, they locked eyes, smiling as the blue of his pupils captured the mesmerizing, dark brown shade of Evelyn's eyes, souls touching as they began to discover one another beyond the surface through their private gaze. Unsure whether it was appropriate to hug or shake hands, the two of them opted to uncomfortably root themselves to the spot. Evelyn had never been looked at like this and her heart began to melt.

"Let me check that number I gave you," Evelyn voiced. He might have some good contacts, she reasoned. She really had nothing to lose. He would be a new industry friend. They could help each other with all things acting she argued with herself.

# # #

As he drove his excited wine fueled friends home, Jack couldn't believe his luck. He smiled at this fortune that fate had presented him. He hadn't fallen for anyone in a long time, surely now would be the time. He would text her before she got in. She was a keeper and her lack of interest proved a challenge.

A short text message conversation continued that evening as they both arrived at their separate homes excited at the prospect of seeing each other the next day.

# # #

Chapter 5

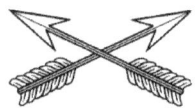

Jack waited patiently as Evelyn excitedly finished her shift behind the bar at the Queens Theatre. The cash was counted from the tills as the fridges were restocked. The lights inside the humming refrigerators were switched to off as the counters were sprayed and wiped clean, ready for the staff that would serve the ticket holders for the show the following evening.

Jack and Evelyn checked their appearances in mirrors at the same time in the adjacent buildings to each other, with an over meticulous vanity that only actors pertain.

"See you tomorrow, Mick!" Evelyn called as she attempted to get her left arm in her jacket, using the other hand to sign out on the hand drawn time sheet placed on an old brown clipboard. A white string spiraled as it held onto the black biro pen for the safe keeping.

"Jack," Evelyn called up to his dressing room window from outside, to which she got no reply.

"JACK!"

A masculine figure appeared at a purposely frosted glass window of the tall red brick wall at the back of the

Gielgud Theatre, frantically fathoming how to open it. He got it slightly ajar, eyes peeping down at Evelyn like a comedy sketch.

"Take this," Jack called back, trying to look as cool as possible as he wedged his strong shoulder in the narrow gap between him and the world outside.

A crisp, twenty pound note floated down from the window as Evelyn watched and tried to catch it in the blustery wind along the cold cobblestones.

The universally recognised face of the Queen Elizabeth, stained with its purple tones, stared up her from the pavement as she retrieved it quickly.

"Go get us a bottle of wine. You choose. I've just got to go back on for the bows and then I'll let you up."

"Where from?"

"Walk up through the little alley, past Madam Jo Jo's and there's a Somerfield or something, try there."

Evelyn walked up the cobbled slope of Soho in the direction of the small supermarket. A glowing smile matching the red tip of her cold nose and cheeks as Soho started to wake up for another exotic evening.

# # #

Armed with a bottle of rich red wine and a bag of Cadbury's chocolate buttons, eating them as she went, Evelyn wandered back towards Jack's theatre. He had seen her coming and raced down the stairs, strategically regaining his cool as he reached the bottom before charmingly greeting Evelyn.

"There she is...!"Jack flirted as Evelyn smiled, silently handing him the plastic bag of goodies.

She didn't know how she had ended up back in his dressing room, but for now she didn't question it. The evening was perfect, they hit it off again, laughing and talking as the talk show host Jonathan Ross interviewed his guests, playing on a portable television screen on Jack's dressing table. The regular activity made believing that they were at home together feasible for a second or two.

The flirting continued and a paramount debate sparked around the topic of the best chocolate bar ever. Jack voting for a Cadbury's Starbar; Evelyn on the side of Cadbury's Clusters, arguably for Jack not entirely a chocolate bar. Neither one had tried the other's favourite so Jack decided an experiment was needed to settle this paramount speculation.

Tomorrow, he decided, he would leave her a gift with her name on it behind the Queen's Theatre stage door.

# # #

It was four-thirty on a late summer afternoon in 2009, and Evelyn Wise braced herself for another mind numbing shift behind the bar. She had spent the morning typing her masters dissertation that was soon to be handed in. On her final approach to the stage door a number of her colleagues stood smoking, leant like smart yobs up against the wall, making the most of their spare time between shows. Today was a double shift; Wednesdays they had a matinee and an evening shift. Evelyn had effortlessly talked her way out of the matinee shift. "There's a parcel for you Evelyn," Mick called over as she chatted to her work mates on the way in.

F.A.O. Miss Evelyn Wise. The black felt tip scribed, handwritten boldly in capital letters on the front of the white package. She opened it with a smile. Inside the large envelope sat silently on clear un popped bubble wrap--a single Starbar.

# # #

For the next three weeks, Wednesday Wine Club became a tradition. Jack throwing down the twenty pounds and Evelyn collecting the goods. They had built a great friendship, but without communicating it both of them wanted more.

Evelyn was confused, she loved her boyfriend and Jack was way too old to enter into a relationship with. There were fourteen years between them however hard they both ignored this. Perhaps this wouldn't be so prevalent later on in life, but right now the thought was unavoidable to both of them.

Evelyn was due to go on holiday and Jack's show was ending. He wouldn't be working next door after next week. She seized the opportunity cooly.

"So can you get tickets for this show of yours then?" Evelyn asked. "I suppose I better see if you're any good or not," she joked.

"Yes, I can get you tickets. When do you want to come?" he replied.

She had worked every night until his show ended, so it really didn't matter which day, as she would have to think of a reason to excuse her self from her shift.

On the selected evening, Evelyn dialed the number for backstage. "Hey Mick, it's Evelyn. Can you tell the managers that I can't make it tonight? I'm not well at all."

"Sure thing ol' girl' you look after yourself. I'll see you soon."

Evelyn and her housemate snuck into the Gielgud Theatre minutes before Jack's show was about to start, careful not to be seen by any of the Queen's Theatre staff, just one door away.

Jack left two tickets behind the desk at the Front of House, seats he had carefully selected so he knew where she would be sitting. Evelyn didn't have a clue what the show was about, although she was excited that she would finally get to see Juliet Carpenter.

Jack had a small role. Stepping on stage, both their hearts sunk. He was nervous she would be watching, and she was unaware that he would be removing his shirt in this seemingly traditional English play.

"Whoa," her eager friend blurted in a hushed tone, nudging Evelyn in the ribs as Jack passionately kissed an actress in front of her. His dreamlike, six-pack chest pressed up against her open white shirt. A pang of unexpected jealously residing in the pit of Evelyn's stomach emerged although she knew it was the nature of his work. The play drew to a close and the company took their bows.

Standing on the front edge of the stage, on the side nearest Evelyn, Jack joined the company as they bowed. The audience applauded enthusiastically from their seats. Jack looked directly at Evelyn as she smiled back, and for that split second, the hundreds of others around them became extinct.

# # #

Chapter 6

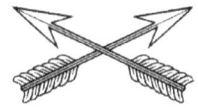

The run of Jack's show drew to a close as the last Wednesday Wine Club approached. Although they intended to see each other again, they knew it would never be like this. As they had done so many times before Jack and Evelyn conversed while sipping their red wine and putting the acting world to rights. They were both aware that tonight would be the last time they would be able to do this as the girl at the Gielgud stage door announced the theatre would be closing in five minutes.

Jack suggested they go for a drink somewhere else. With his bag thrown over his shoulder, he took Evelyn's hand leading her through the cobbled streets to a public house near by. The weekday lust continuing elsewhere.

Starry-eyed, they sipped their drinks. Evelyn was aware that she needed to catch the last train, that was unless Jack wanted to drive her home so she could stay with him a bit longer. Jack lived in Essex, the opposite side of London to Evelyn. Not leaving it too late, he chose to drive her home. Evelyn's apartment was set back off the main Finchley Road, the emergency exit iron stairs, framing the older looking London building like a movie set in a back alley of New York.

He walked her up to her door as she gave him the grand tour of the small, fairly empty three-bedroom apartment. She was due to be home alone this evening. The bathroom door was opened as he peaked inside. Then, leading him down the short corridor, Evelyn showed Jack her room, briefly, not wanting him to go in.

Her feelings for him building every second they spent together, knowing it wasn't right, knowing she had an honest and loving boyfriend who would be there for her through it all. Jack watched her, mesmerized, not taking in his surroundings at all, only captured by her energy and suppressing every urge in his pent up body to kiss every inch of her youthful figure.

The apartment was silent as the evening crept towards the early hours of morning. Neighboring flats had turned their lights out hours before. Turning back to exit her room, Jack embraced the privacy they had never had before. He grabbed the sides of her face, passionately kissing her for the first time before leading her onto her bed.

His lips retold the way he had felt over the last few weeks. The kissing continued without a word. Neither one of them had kissed someone for such an extended period of time. Evelyn's kisses with her boyfriend had become a quick, habitual snog and Jack had not felt this close to a women in years. Hours passed as they connected through the touch of their mouths, the sun beginning to peak through the dusty blinds, as fully clothed, they fell asleep in the innocence of each other's arms.

#It was different finishing work knowing Jack would never smile out of that particular dressing room window again. Evelyn still looked up fondly, imagining him there once more, a warm glow radiating in her heart.

Jack began a new routine, declining the option to continue the show as a tour around theatres in the country and turning his attention to his next acting chapter. Jack hit the gym hard, a haven to refocus, his work outs strengthening his mind and body, as he prepared to hit the audition circuit again.

A planned summer holiday was approaching for Evelyn. They had spoke to each other most days, but Evelyn had yet to tell Jack that she would be out of the country next week. Waiting for a big red London bus to take her home, her Oyster card at the ready, her mobile phone rang from her bag.

Diving into her deep handbag, she finally located the ringing phone. Jack's name flashed up on her home screen and she answered it, happy to hear from him. Jack was excited to arrange plans to meet her, wanting to organise a dinner date together the following week.

"I can't make next week unfortunately as I am going on holiday," she answered chirpily.

Unaware of these exotic plans led Jack to consequently ask, "Who with?" Thinking on her feet, she lied. "The girls."

He could hear the dishonesty in her voice. She should be a good liar, pretending, otherwise known as acting, was what she had spent her entire education mastering. "You have a boyfriend, don't you?" Silence stunned the line.

"Evelyn, are you going away on holiday with your boyfriend?"

Scared to lose him, she reluctantly confessed, "Yes."

# # #

Evelyn left for her European vacation, excited for a break and hopeful she may be able to reignite things with her current boyfriend. They had been together a while and although it had been fun to spend time with Jack, she felt secure in this relationship. Her boyfriend knew her, properly, inside and out. However, unwanted private thoughts of Jack helplessly entered her mind.

She loved two people and for her own peace of mind, a decision had to be made. She had to let go of the relationship she was in. Habit, society and their friendship had bound her in a tight grip. The week-long vacation had come to a conclusion and as the couple departed for a different flights, Evelyn tightly hugged her boyfriend and best friend goodbye.

Watching him leave, she knew in her gut she would never see him again. She retired to the public airport restrooms, confining herself to a cubicle as the pain of heartache washed over her like a tidal wave and the tears followed. She had been a coward. Letting him leave with false hope of the relationship sustaining, the truth imprisoned from leaving her lips.

As she returned home to Heathrow Airport, turning on her mobile phone, which had been unable to retain signal abroad, an alert of a text message appeared: "Jack: Welcome back. I hope you had a good trip."

# # #

Chapter 7

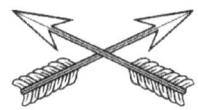

It wasn't long after she had unpacked, before Jack came over to visit Evelyn at her Finchley Road flat. Armed with a new DVD and a heart melting smile, he knocked on the door and they settled in for an evening together, building a den with the sofas in the bare, student-like living room.

Alone in the apartment for the evening. Jack had brought round "Milk," starring Sean Penn, for them to watch. The film ran on the television as Jack's arm sneaked around Evelyn as they relaxed in their surroundings. The pair were distracted from the film running in front of them, the chemistry of energy flowing electrically between them as they kissed their way onto the floor.

Evelyn lay under Jack as he kissed her intensely. Their bodies pressed together, feeling each other's excitement under the restriction of their clothing. Evelyn controlled the sexually heated situation by vowing nothing more could happen whilst she was still in a relationship. Moving back to the safety of the sofa, they focussed on the film although their mind wandered, now sexually stirred.

# # #

Chapter 8

The humidity of the sea side summer air was just right. A tall, dark-haired man was mowing the grass in a large, back garden with a small mower, which he guided in football pitch lines, professionally striping the lavish greenery. The basic task offered him a chance to escape his busy mind rather than think about money or what Evelyn was doing. Inner peace. Just him and his garden in the sunshine, the smell of his freshly cut lawn, the enjoyable aroma in the air.

Evelyn had never been to Jack's house and he was excited for her visit. It wasn't that he kept it untidy, but the clean up that was in full swing was long overdue. Kicking off his flip-flops, which were now covered in fresh grass cuttings, he headed in the back door to start on tidying up inside. A large, black bin bag gathered up empty cartons and wrappers that lay about the lounge.

Freshly washed bedding was taken upstairs and upon leaving the room with the bed now made, he located a hidden key to another room. As the key turned, Jack prized the stiff door, which opened out onto an iron door situated behind it. He unbolted it carefully, passing through a black curtain into a disguised lair. The door closed carefully behind him.

After ten minutes he came out, strategically locking one door after the other behind him and returning to his romantic preparations. Returning downstairs, Jack straightened the blanket thrown over the back of the three seater sofa before sitting back to admire the newly reformed cleanliness he had created.

# # #

The Tube was particularly busy with suits and shirts today as Evelyn plugged her Ipod Nano into her ears to accompany her on her journey to ultimately meet Jack. Having spoke to each other continuously since they met, she had not yet visited his house. They were going to get a drink (to calm both their nerves) and then would go back to his house. It would be late by then and the question of staying the night loomed.

She hadn't been with anyone sexually, other than the boyfriend she had had since University and the unknown idea of another man's hands on her slight body made her anxious.

The arrangement had been made to pick Evelyn up from a leisure centre where she was entertaining at a children's party, a job she did alongside her bar job at Les Miserables to fund her acting pursuits.

Jack pulled up in an old, open-top black Jeep he had been fixing on cue from Evelyn's exit from the leisure centre, the time synchronized, as it often was when they joined forces. They locked eyes, feeling at home in their hearts once more as the young girl crossed the road to meet the hauntingly good looking older man, who wore a black baseball cap and stood beside his car in the blazing late summer sunshine.

Each new meeting took them awhile to settle into each other's company. Maybe because it wasn't as regularly as they would like to have seen each other, maybe because they were both fighting for survival in their own lives and letting their guards down usually came at a price. Nevertheless, after the initial de centering, the blood began to rush through them once more and the craving began.

Jack drove the car through a council owned housing estate as Evelyn denied the unease that began to creep up to her throat from the pit of her stomach. He hadn't said they were going somewhere else first.

"Wait in the car a minute," Jack affirmed, pulling the open top black Jeep over opposite a run down pub, a refuge for the residents in the area.

It wasn't the ideal start that Evelyn had hoped for in her mind. Denying her faithful instincts, the voice of her mother and the phrase "no one's perfect" danced in her head as she waited patiently. Only one friend of Evelyn's really knew about Jack, who she contemplated contacting and considered against it. Mainly because of the age gap and the instinctual knowing that it wasn't right for her to be visiting him, let alone entertaining the idea of his chest pressed up against hers. She chose to keep the information close to her heart.

After a long twenty minutes, Jack returned, suspiciously placing something in the locked middle compartment of the car, instructing Evelyn to get out and join him in the pub. Things were going to take longer than he had initially anticipated.

A tall bottle of rose wine stood in the middle of a round black wooden table, surrounded by four stumpy bar stools with dark tattered velvet cushions, which mirrored the empty dive of a pub. The label on the pink bottle was cold from its refrigeration, dew drops clinging to the glass.

The pub was dark, and the rough regulars were taken aback by Evelyn's youthful beauty, a stranger to these parts and noticeably unarmed. From the other side of the room strolled a white man, skinny with cheap unoriginal commercial tattoos, his head shaven. The man cautiously sat down next to Jack's intimidatingly trained frame as Evelyn began pouring the wine. With care she filled the two short bowl shaped wine goblets, water marked from the dirty pub's dishwasher residue. The answer to this uneasy situation was confidently resolved in the liquid Jack and Evelyn now sipped.

After a brief conversation, the tattooed man and Jack moved without conversation to another part of the pub to discuss privately the matter in question, leaving Evelyn alone with the wine. Her instincts never failed her and she knew that she would be pleased to be leaving this place sooner rather than later.

Jack spoke in a strong, but hushed manner.

"I really don't give two..." He restrained himself from swearing. "Find the money within the next ten minutes. By the time we finish that bottle, you will be back with the cash."

He was losing his patience and consequently his home, rapidly. He looked over at Evelyn completely unaware of the intensity of his circumstances and smiled it off. Sitting like a slice of innocence and beautiful naiveté accidentally mixed up in his madness.

The clock in the pub ticked as Jack sat silently focused, adrenaline pumping through him. He had to get this cash, his phone had not stopped ringing for days and he had lost count of the amount of threatening red letters he had received with requests of money he owed through his letterbox. If only he could share this burdening black cloud with Evelyn. But she was perfect, the only good thing he had going on right now and the last thing he wanted was to ruin the heroic image she had of him. Even though he knew with her intelligence, she would have her rightful suspicions. He would remain controlled. He had dealt with far worse than this. He wrapped his arm around his new love and kissed her softly on her forehead not wanting to worry her.

The bottle of pink liquid was three quarters of the way empty when Jack acknowledged the signal from the tattooed bald man and went outside. Collecting Evelyn on his return, he hurried her back into the aging jeep, pocketing the cash, his nerves stabilized for another day.

# # #

Chapter 9

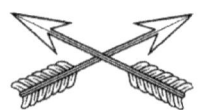

Evelyn watched Jack's strong shoulders relax as they drove out of the estate and back onto the open dual carriageway. The English countryside dissolving the harsh graffitied brick of the council estate they had left behind as he reassuringly rested his hand on her thigh closest to him.

Jack and Evelyn were very similar in their ways. Both fueled with energy and osmotic happiness when things were going their way, but silenced and shut down to regain control when life caught them off guard.

They left the dual carriageway, speeding over road humps with the music blaring, adding to the fire of the alcohol they had drunk. They entered a small town on the outskirts of East london, lined with bars and restaurants where Jack pulled up on double, yellow lines outside a vibrantly sexy cocktail bar.

The couple got out, excited to start their evening together. Jack joked with the bar tender who was pleased to see him and placed an order for two Champagne cocktails. They both loved a drink, a device to block out the struggle. It was the only way they knew how. It also released the nerves they had around each other at this early stage. Topping up the rose wine they had drunk in the previous pub, the champagne cocktails came one after the other as they talked between flirtatious kisses.

The drinks and date merriment continued to flow. Evelyn become increasingly unaware of her consumption. Jack was proud to show her off and made the executive decision to leave this cocktail bar and romance his new love on their fun bar crawl across the street. Greeting the bouncers at the door, Jack waited whilst Evelyn's I.D was consulted.

"Thanks mate, have a good night; look after her," the bouncer bantered to Jack.

Entering the bar, Jack lost Evelyn, whose eye sight was beginning to blur. She had set off to find the nearest woman's toilet. Jack sat at a table in the garden area and ordered another bottle of rose wine for the two of them to enjoy and waited for her return. Looking at his phone he questioned whether to reply to a text from his agent requesting him to visit her at home. He must have fallen for Evelyn to be ignoring this fateful demand.

# # #

In the bathroom Evelyn stared at the mirror attempting to refocus herself. After topping up her lipgloss, she drunkenly decided the only way through this was to continue drinking to escape the guilt she carried for her unfaithful actions and the uncertainty she felt for Jack.

Programmed with an unconscious knowing of how to behave when drunk, a theory she had not yet tested on a date, really only in holiday nightclubs in Europe with her friends, she began to walk in a straight line towards the men at the bar.

Evelyn approached a group of young lads, excited by a single woman showing them attention. Evelyn confidently sipped their drinks as she spoke to them, looking for Jack. Stabilizing herself against the bar, she knocked into a pint of Fosters lager, which crashed to the ground. The shattering spillage alerted the bouncers.

"Fucking stupid bitch," one of the boys cursed as Evelyn tried to apologise.

Grabbing her firmly by both arms, the bouncers hauled her from the bar as Jack got up from the garden to see what was going on. His eyes darted to the door as one of the doorman told him to sort out his bird, who was now a disgrace on the pavement.

Evelyn laughed nervously as Jack's blood raged. In his embarrassment he scooped Evelyn up, placing her in the car without a word. The engine of the Jeep roared as Evelyn struggled with her seatbelt and Jack sped towards the nearest tube station.

The silence was deafening as they arrived at a small train station as Jack raised his voice to Evelyn.

"Get out of my car," he announced.

"What?" With her mind spinning Evelyn was only just beginning to realize the dramatic change in her situation.

"There's the station. Go home," Jack fumed.

"No," Evelyn stated firmly.

Through gritted teeth Jack threatened menacingly, "Get. Out. Of. My car... NOW." Jack threw her overnight bag into the station car park. "You want it?"

Evelyn didn't answer, willing herself to sober up. He had a temper that was beginning to scare her.

Jack's anger grew as a sense of sheer disappointment set in. Evelyn was the first women he had fallen for in years, but her immature behavior enraged him. The driver side door swung open as he launched himself out of the car and around to the passenger door. If she wouldn't get out, he would get her out.

Frightened, head spinning from copious amounts of alcohol, Evelyn locked the passenger door as Jack tried to open it, angering him even further.

"Open this door right now!"

Still Evelyn refused.

Finally, reaching over the open top roof of the old Jeep, Jack grabbed her under the arms knocking her carelessly on the metal frame of the vehicle as she fell down a grass verge against a corrugated iron fence pleading with him as he sped off.

# # #

Chapter 10

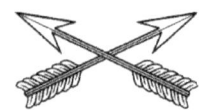

A very silent two weeks passed between them. Neither one wanted to be the first to contact the other and apologise after what had happened.

One missed call listed on the home screen of her mobile and Evelyn's phone rang again. Frustrated, she answered: "I'm done Jack. I don't do second chances. Sorry."

"Oh, go on," Jack teased hopefully.

"No, sorry. I don't have any feelings for you. I shouldn't have seen you anyway. I have learnt my lesson."

"One more...?" Jack teased.

"No."

"What if I took you to a theme park tomorrow? A fun day just you and me?"

"I'm not interested. Sorry." Evelyn put the phone down. She really was done with him and his erratic behavior. Goodbye and good luck.

He had never given up so easily before and wasn't about to start. A charming and playful text campaign began. A few hours later, Evelyn answered the phone to Jack again.

Without letting him speak she announced, "I'll come to the theme park if you're paying. Bring the best picnic and don't you dare be late or I promise you I will not come out of my house. Deal?"

"Deal."

With that Evelyn hung up continuing with her planned evening activities. Jack smiled to himself. The game continuing.

# # #

He woke up at five a.m. the next morning, dressing quickly as he looked forward to the fun day ahead. It would take him an hour to get to her house and then they would drive three hours to the park.

Evelyn looked at the clock, willing herself out of bed as the covers somehow crept back over her head. Her housemates were not yet up for work as she packed a bag for the day, peeking through the blinds in her room for Jack's arrival. She was serious that if he was even a minute late she would go back to bed.

But in fact, Jack arrived five minutes early, texting her to come down. Evelyn smiled to herself, locking the door behind her and climbing down the steel fire escape to join a smug looking Jack in the car.

The roads were fairly empty as they reached the motorway and the heightened awareness of the close proximity to each other lingered in the air. After an hour or so, Evelyn was finally fully awake as Jack drove peacefully and they set about to look for somewhere on route that served a wholesome, cooked breakfast.

Finding a perfect place, they settled in. A perfectly cooked fried egg, sausage, back bacon, fried bread and spoonful of Heinz baked beans looked loving back up at them from the solid white plates. The usually early morning wake up for both of them making their mouths water at the sight as the crisp bacon smell wafted towards them. Tucking in to their breakfasts, Jack complimented his with brown sauce, while Evelyn doused hers with tomato ketchup.

Returning to the compact car to continue the romantic road trip, Evelyn retrieved a CD she had packed from her bag and announced that she had a car competition for them. Playfully, she put the track forward to number seventeen, as the introduction to Bill Withers' "Lovely Day" began to build up through the speakers.

"Right, these are the rules." Evelyn announced bossily. "Basically, it's whoever can hold the note the longest without taking a breath. The dayyyyyyy pretty much gets longer every time he says it."

"You're on!" Jack replied.

Their faces were serious, staring strongly out of the front windscreen determined to win. Both of them had competed at sports to a high level and were not easily defeated. The deep breath taken just before the "day" made the other laugh as they began choking on the gasps of air they took in, in preparation for the elongated word, vocalizing it for as long as their lungs would allow them to.

Jack proudly won the first round. His championship reigned for the rest of the journey, as he boastfully teased Evelyn about her loss.

The road signs announced they weren't too far away from the amusement park as Jack turned onto a country lane off the main dual carriageway. A small country shop provided the perfect stop for snacks. As they pondered in the shop, Jack and Evelyn's accents were now somewhat different from the shopkeepers.

Jumping back in the car they arrived at the park. The car bumping along the graveled road, Jack parking as instructed by an arm waving attendant into their allocated space for the day.

# # #

With his backpack braced, Jack held Evelyn as they queued for the monorail to take them to the ticket booth. The uneasy feeling of prying eyes that watched them as they held each other happily in the line highlighted to them the appearance of the age gap--something they were already overly conscious of.

Among the roller coasters of this particular park stood a picturesque castle, the rides racing around the green grounds. Jack and Evelyn climbed the tower clambering over the no entry signs and out onto the forted terrace. The top terrace was built up high, arrow slits peeking through the archaic stone walls as they explored the rooftop. They could see the entire park from up here.

Alone and above the gaze of the public, perusing the park, Jack took Evelyn's hand and pulled her close to him, their eyes locking once more as he held her tightly in his arms holding her face as he kissed her sweetly out of sight.

The rest of the park was buzzing below, the excited children running with open maps as they headed towards the next ride. Breaking away from the privacy of their kiss Jack kept Evelyn close.

"We could get married here, invite all our friends, hire the entire park for the day... how cool would that be?" Jack whispered, wrapping his coat around her in his arms.

Evelyn assumed he was joking, but for a moment she allowed herself to fall in love with the idea, blissfully entertaining the fun thoughts of married life with him, before brushing it away to protect her heart.

Jack was an adventurer and decided even after paying the fee for both of them to get into the park that the woodland and gardens between the parks were of far more interest than the commercial rides. The gardens were beautiful. Perfectly trimmed, naturally vibrant green, hedged walls and grey stoned statues lined the colourfully pruned floral estate gardens.

As Evelyn and Jack walked hand in hand, her mobile phone rang and her boyfriend's name flashed up on the screen. She stood staring at it before walking away from Jack and taking the call.

# # #

Chapter 11

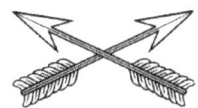

Jack watched her hand leave his as she headed off, leaving Jack to question what he was doing here. He could only go with this moment and the pure feelings he couldn't describe that lingered continuously in his heart for her.

It wasn't that Evelyn didn't love her boyfriend, she knew what she was doing was wrong and that a future with Jack was almost impossible. She already had a stable relationship with a kind man, who would never hurt her. The guilt emanated throughout her body.

He had called to say he had read her final university papers and had emailed her with feedback. She hurried off the phone, lying that she had to get back to the library. Her heart tore in two.

# # #

"Everything ok?" Jack asked curiously.

"Yes" she half smiled, taking his hand again to reassure him physically that she wanted to be here with him. They grabbed some lunch, he hadn't prepared a picnic at Evelyn's request, but had managed to worm his way out with his charms, and they sat by the water with some rather tasty take away food.

A herd of excited Canadian Geese waddled over at the optimistic prospect of a free lunch. Jack sat calmly undisturbed by them as Evelyn ran away nervously with her food, Jack watching her with a smile.

The afternoon became jam packed with activities, fast tracking to the front of the lines of the best rides as they chatted continuously. Their day had been sensational, and, as the sunlight began to fade, hundreds of guests followed the signs towards the park exit. They drove back as the sun set. Evelyn snoozing, her head resting on the passenger seat window.

Jack admired her innocently as she rested. It was dark by the time they arrived back at Evelyn's house. Gently waking her, Jack kissed Evelyn on her forehead.

"Thank you for the best day," she said softly. Jack took her in his arms as they embraced and Evelyn exited the car for the evening.

Climbing the New York resembling fire exit staircase sleepily, Evelyn opened her front door. Sitting cross-legged on her bed, she noticed she was content, but somewhat torn. Evelyn could feel herself falling for Jack. This wasn't just a bit of fun anymore. Noticing her womanly instincts she had begun considering a committed relationship with Jack. She began to dial her boyfriend's number. The time had come for a much needed confession.

# # #

Chapter 12

It was five days before Christmas. Jack blew the horn of a white van, another vehicle Evelyn had not seen before. Crossing the street, she jumped in as quickly as she could, the snow was beginning to fall faster now than it had been when she had left her apartment to catch the train. She looked back at the tube station entrance wondering whether they would be running later this evening if the weather continued the way it was at present. Walking across in the snow to meet Jack, who was smiling with the window down, she questioned how she would get home later if the trains weren't running.

Jack blasted the heating for her on her arrival into the van, giving her a passionate kiss on the lips and kindly rubbing her wet thighs in an effort to warm her up and comfort her from the dreaded public transport journey.

"You alright, little one?" he asked with a glow of happiness in his voice.

"I am now," she replied with a cheeky grin leaving her lips. Evelyn kissed him softly on the back of his neck as he melted to her loving touch. Home at last.

# # #

Leaving their meeting point, the weather conditions worsened as the snow fell faster than Jack's van's window wipers could clear it and the traffic began to pile up in front of them. Normally, this would be a dreadful situation for anyone, but the danger that they may have to sleep in the van until the snow passed only added to the magic of this moment. Evelyn would have to stay with Jack tonight. Even if they turned around now, the traffic back to the station would be so heavy, that they may not get there in time. The van radio reported the treacherous conditions and public transport closures that plagued Evelyn's mind.

Jack was pleased she would have to stay; he had longed to wake up next to her for weeks. He looked ahead with a wealth of inner peace as he eased the van onto the slip road of a merging dual carriageway. It was during their car journeys that Evelyn and Jack learnt the most about each other and this trip proved fruitful in its discoveries.

The van heaters warmed Evelyn in her seat as Jack rested his hand on her thigh. She leaned in towards him, her head rested on his side whilst he drove. It was funny, they never could get close enough. Jack wrapped his arm around her, his other hand firmly on the steering wheel. The traffic wasn't moving fast and the couple were now aching to relieve their bladders. Finally, they were able to get off the dual carriageway as the van's headlights struggled with the mounting snow that was now settling.

Jack parked the car on the side of the road, scooting round the other side to help Evelyn, laughing as they went, slipping and sliding on ice as they looked for somewhere secluded to alleviate themselves. The wet snow surface was super slippery as they ice skated across it trying not to fall over.

"This task is going to be a lot easier for you than me," laughed Evelyn, her feet sinking into the snow as she walked.

# # #

Three hours later, they arrived back at Jack's house following their journey that would normally have only taken an hour-and-a-half. It was dark now, the light having faded early, as the cold days drew shorter in the depths of winter. Having not planned to stay, Evelyn had only one bag, which Jack carried in for her, slung over his rugged shoulder as the couple made their way into his house for the first time.

His house was bigger than Evelyn had imagined, although he had told her it was a house and not an apartment somehow she had only pictured something small. It was grand in its appearance and she could feel the sea breeze hit her face as he opened the back door to show Evelyn the large garden space, illuminating in front of her as Jack turned on the outside lights.

It was getting late, but going to bed now would be a difficult topic to approach. Her nervousness of being in his space and not hers led Evelyn to make uneducated and obvious statements about the objects Jack housed. They settled in, Jack welcoming her warmly into his homey space.

Jack was not frequently visited by others in his home and suggested a late night game of pool, which their competitive spirits became enthused by. Grabbing their own cues for the challenge, a new rule Jack had invented was explained, the laws clearly lain down. Jack suggested using difficult body parts to steer their cues and pocket the balls on the table. Proving to be a professional, he pocketed one yellow ball after the other, Evelyn laughing in amusement as he wrapped himself in what could only be described as self invented yoga poses around the felt green table.

When finished, Jack lit the tall cream candles in his lounge and they sat drinking hot seasonal mulled wine, complete with cinnamon sticks and a shot of Jack's insistent orange liquor to give it a Christmas kick. A perfect silence calmed them as they drank their 'hot toddies' sleepily in the flickering candle light.

"I'll stay down here on the sofa tonight when you want to go to bed," Jack reassured her.

"Don't be silly; it's your bed. I really don't mind staying on the sofa...or, we can both sleep upstairs. I think we are capable of lying next to one another without touching," Evelyn joked.

# # #

He reassured her that he would take her all the way home once the tubes reopened and the snow had cleared.

Borrowing one of his t-shirts, sleeping safely in her chastity leggings, Evelyn instinctively found the empty side of Jack's gigantic bed. Jack, who usually slept relatively unclothed, nervously lay next to her in a t-shirt and a pair of comfy jogging bottoms, rolling over to face the wall, his heart racing as he turned out the light and wished Evelyn good night in a friendly tone.

After everything that had happened, they had both convinced themselves that they could only be friends and that it was wrong for them to want more. The age gap of fourteen years forever present in both their minds. Try as they might, they were unable to change how they felt towards each other. Laying in the dark room, an overpowering stillness silenced them.

Evelyn rolled towards Jack, unconsciously asking him to face inwards. He knew he shouldn't; she was nearly half his age, but before he could answer his turmoiling ego, their eyes locked. The whites of their pupils were the only light in the room other than the concentrated illumination of the moon that shone beyond the window in the winter sky. Staring at each other, hearts thundering through their chests, Jack took Evelyn by the hand. The cosmic energy radiated through each of them as their lips met under the heavy duvet and they made love for the first time.

# # #

Chapter 13

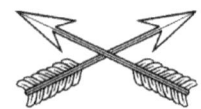

Morning broke with the flickering of the sun's rays and the fresh sea air blew softly into the room from the open window. Peace. After a late night, the two of them lay peacefully in the queen-sized bed.

Jack's hand reached behind him to find Evelyn's, whose fingers responded to his touch, palms connecting. He rolled over looking at her soft blonde hair resting on a pillow beside him. Spooning her toasty body, he gently pushed her hair behind her ear, before kissing slowly down the trail of her silky, olive skin.

Her youth and unscathed innocence captured him. He had never been with a woman so much younger than himself, a girl even, but she was unlike anyone he had met before. She was fearless and didn't need his protection. Or so he thought, and she was fun, he always laughed with Evelyn.

He kissed her innocently each one physically confessing his attachment to her whilst he watched her beautiful body relax even further to the touch of his lips against her toned lower abs, the outside world fading again as the ocean breeze blew in from the open window and the ecstasy continued.

Jack ran Evelyn a hot bath before pottering around in the kitchen whilst Evelyn wrapped herself in his covers. Her small body was lost in the huge bed as Jack prepared their porridge. From the bedroom Evelyn called to Jack who was now in the bathroom upstairs moisturizing his face.

"Is this the bit where your wife comes home and tells me to get out of her bed?" Evelyn joked.

"Yes, she will be back in a bit. You better hurry up," Jack teased.

Evelyn pushed her small feet against the bottom of the bath tub her knees raising as her happy, make-up free face was covered in the hot water. Jack sat on the bathroom floor, leaning against the radiator with a cup of coffee. Jack's dog settled at his feet as he stroked the crown of his companion's head contentedly, watching Evelyn enjoy a relaxing soak.

The house was filled with a happy silence. They really didn't have a lot in the grand scheme of material things. Their combined monetary values ever deprecating in their accounts, but this moment for Jack was worth more than anything. Just the three of them, loving family unit, safe in his home.

They polished off their porridge and snuggled down for an afternoon in each other's arms. The snow that had fallen the night before meant that the roads continued to be off limits today.

# # #

After the roads were de-iced, Jack drove Evelyn home. They continued to meet as regular as their own acting pursuits made it possible. With the advantage of his age, Jack unknowingly introduced Evelyn to a number of new things. Although she was physically attracted to him, Evelyn's attraction always grew from the things that he taught her and the encouragement he gave her to pursue her dreams.

On this particular lunchtime meet up, the new adventure was sushi. Introducing her to something new was a technique he had read about from his trusty companion on dating woman, a book called "The Game." Screwing her nose up at the prospect of rice and raw fish for lunch, instead of three luxury exquisitely filled mini rolls from Marks and Spencer (her usual choice), Jack encouraged her to dip her toe into new waters. The initially repelled look that had dominated her face before the ladened chopstick arrived anywhere close to her mouth was soon replaced when the California roll reluctantly appeased her appetite.

Jack looked on in amusement at her surprised enjoyment. With the soy sauce all dipped out, Evelyn and Jack left their lunch date and continued their individual days formally timetabled with separate acting classes in Central London.

# # #

Jack collected Evelyn from the tube station and they grabbed a Chinese takeaway bringing it back to Jack's, the car perfumed with the smell of oriental fast food. The bag rested on Evelyn's lap as she picked at the prawn crackers on the way back.

Jack had moved his bed downstairs. His bright idea to expand his incriminating space upstairs had been started sporadically as the idea entered Jack's mind without thinking it through as he had jumped right in and started the task without much other thought.

Tonight they would sleep downstairs, a surprising discovery as Evelyn turned the corner of the kitchen to locate the sofa which was still in its rightful place with the bed behind it at the other end of the room. She laughed to herself before asking Jack what this was all about.

The Chinese treat filled them as a food slumber followed and they snuggled in front of the television, Evelyn dosing in his muscular arms as the screen flickered in front of them.

# # #

The next morning was set for an outdoor fitness pursuit. They both loved their fitness and today Evelyn had said she would complete a run Jack had been suggesting for a while.

Loading the dog in the car, Jack and Evelyn sat side by side in their jogging attire. Trainers poised for the sporting pursuit ahead. After a twenty minute drive or so, Jack turned the car into a small muddied car park opposite a country pub. Clambering out of the small car, Jack let his dog out from the back seat who was very familiar with this run, scrambling ahead to mark their territory.

Their fitness levels were above average, endurance at its optimum as they snaked through the woods side by side, muddying their shoes. Reaching an open space ahead, Jack pointed to a hill that would be the next stage in this morning's activity. Heartbreak Hill.

"If you can get to the top without stopping you won't get your heartbroken," he confidently proclaimed through controlled, but heavy breathing.

"Deal" Evelyn replied.

Presently tired from the ground they had already covered Evelyn's determination was not about to wilt at this stage. She, like Jack, loved a challenge.

The hill stood like a mountain as Evelyn gazed up at it. A deep breath was taken and the hill was defeated. An overwhelming satisfaction prevailing as they enjoyed freely running down the other side. Jack looked on, proud of her, as Evelyn ran from start to finish without stopping.

In an effort to display this sense of pride on his woman's achievements he walked over in an effort to give her a cuddle as she crossed the imaginary finish line back near where they had parked the car. This was positively declined by Evelyn as her body urged her to catch her breath, Jack watching in amusement.

After driving back, Jack ran her a ritual morning bath to soak her muscles, filled with bubbles for his little beauty. A large white towel warmed itself on the radiator. Exiting the bath Evelyn was comforted with it, her refreshed, toned physique snuggling up as her long, naked legs made her way into the bedroom to dress. Evelyn watched him unlock a bolt through the crack in their bedroom door.

Jack was aware of her curious gaze as she looked on, innocently wrapped in her towel. Drying her hair in her fitted black underwear, she became overly curious about his mysterious actions from the furniture-less room she now got ready in. Now dressed, Evelyn made her way down the uncarpeted stairs for breakfast as Jack called her back up.

"Evelyn, come here little one, I want to show you something."

Making her way back up after his request she saw him smiling like a cheshire cat outside the bolted door.

"Yes...?" she asked sexily reaching the landing.

"Come and look at this. I want you to see something."

The room which Evelyn really hadn't taken much notice of before, having assumed it was a spare bedroom, was unlocked before her. Another door appeared behind the false facade. A latch at the top was unbolted. As the couple walked through, Evelyn's eyes opened to a sight she couldn't have even imagined.

"A little sideline," he announced. The room was hot and extremely bright, exposing white lamps that shone down onto a wealth of greenery. The smell illegal. She wasn't impressed, smiling through the danger that crept through her bones. She needed to leave.

# # #

Chapter 14

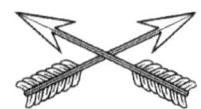

Evelyn walked out of the room without a word as Jack pottered in the incriminating space before sitting down with a pair of scissors to prepare the Cannabis for a customer.

"Are you going to help me then?" Jack joked, secretly hoping she would.

"No," Evelyn replied with confidence and walked back down the stairs leaving Jack to question this money making habit that had somehow become normality.

The afternoon left stale remnants of the newly discovered information as they made love that evening. Their addictive craving for each other dismissed any other thoughts. Calm and sexually satisfied, they slept.

A loud ringing resonated in the room in the early hours of the morning. They were awoken in the night by a call that rang in on Jack's mobile. The caller talked with empathy as Jack listened, one word answers leaving Jack's lips, a concern growing as he answered the caller in his tired voice.

The call ended and Jack lay deadly silent, Evelyn beside him internally questioning whether he was okay. She knew he wasn't. Reassuringly and softly touching his side, Evelyn noticed his world had just been rocked.

She silently took him in her arms. For the first time, she became the protection he so desperately sought. Laying closer to one an other, Jack described the news of a close friend of his who had just passed away. The news having just been parted to him on the recent telephone call. An emptiness materialized, emotion draining from the usually fun-filled man, radiating through the now hollow structure of his trained physique. The burial would be tomorrow.

# # #

The morning sunshine broke, pouring into the house, as Evelyn sat on the bottom step of the painted white wooden staircase, placing her black sock into a green wellington boot. Jack was very quiet today, reflective and subdued as expected, Evelyn looking on for the first time as his vulnerability was exposed.

She had often convinced herself he was a monster, no good for her, unconventional and entirely unsuitable for what she needed, but in this state, his wounds reflected why they were magnetized to each other. They both wanted to be loved so much, without the tools to ask for it.

They walked across the marshland and out towards the sea, a five minute stroll before the mighty English ocean was once more in sight. As the dog ran up ahead, the wind raced around Jack and Evelyn looking towards each other with a caring smile. Fresh faced from the walk, they returned to his house, Evelyn packing up her belongings as Jack dug out his suit for the funeral.

Shirtless, he began to iron his funeral attire as Evelyn took in his vulnerable state; she had never seen him like this. She willingly rescued him in his domestic pursuit.

Without a word she took the iron smiling, steaming and starching the now crisp collar. Buttoning his shirt for him, she kissed him softly as she reached the top, folding down his collar, smiling at him with kind eyes to reassure him he was loved. No other man could have achieved this domestic bliss from Evelyn. She was wholly independent and didn't need a man, in her mind anyway.

He bent to tie his shoes as she placed her bag in his car, both unaware of the older woman next door who appeared at her open window as Jack drove the car out of the drive.

# # #

Chapter 15

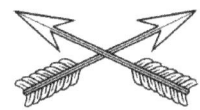

Evelyn had got them two tickets, a surprise for Jack. He paid for everything they did and she wanted to do something for him. When she presented the theatre tickets to him, they revealed to be front row seats for the production of War Horse that was showing at The New London Theatre. Neither of them had seen the show before and it had remarkable views in all the papers.

Entering the theatrical venue hand in hand, the tannoy system speakers announced: "Ladies and Gentlemen, can you please take your seats as this evening's performance will commence in five minutes."

The show was magnificent as they thoroughly enjoyed the heartwarming story retold on stage before them. Their hands remaining in comforted contact throughout the show, breaking on occasion to reward the actors with their rapturous applause. The standing ovation they, and the rest of the audience joined in, which physically announced their gratitude for such a marvelously performed piece.

As they walked back to the car, Jack told Evelyn he wanted to ask her something. Taking his time, Jack skirted around the topic, coming back to his point a few fumbling minutes later.

"Would you like to come to my sister's wedding with me? I would love to have you as my guest."

Evelyn was grateful to be asked. "I would love too," she replied with a smile as he kissed her back in response. The formal occasion marked a seemingly committed step forward in the growth of their relationship.

# # #

A week passed, the couple enjoying long phone calls in the evenings whilst they lay outstretched on their individual beds. Jack's illegal sideline was his private business, Evelyn naively decided. She loved being with him and knew, given time, his acting career would take off and this would be left behind, or so she thought.

Jack napped on the sofa as Evelyn fidgeted in his arms trying to get comfy on the single strand of the three seater sofa that Jack had taken up most of. She nestled in a small niche she found on the inside as Jack wrapped his spare arm around her, kissing her forehead in an unconscious reassurance that the space was a great find. They fitted together like a puzzle piece, not many other couples could both fit on a sofa like this.

In need of some fresh air after their nap, Jack drove them down the road to a old wooden seaside pier. The pillars were cemented in the wet, cement like sand, covered in a history of green and black seaweed. The pier was not far from Jack's house. Walking hand in hand, they made their way to the end of it to watch the fishermen in their pursuits. The tremendous waves crashed onto the British beach and the wind blew around them, their faces receiving a rosy glow from the crisp chill.

The pier was ever so long and some visitors chose to ride the miniature railway train that went back and forth loading and unloading passengers at each end of the wooden structure. The track was laid historically, the laddered steel shining in the sunlight as Jack and Evelyn's faces filled with smiles. Reaching the end of the slatted wooden structure that was continually being weathered under their feet, Evelyn let go of Jack's hand, her childlike curiosity overwhelming her to adventure.

She leaned over the edge as the wind blew through her hair and she looked out towards the English Channel. The end of the pier was slightly slippery from the rain as Evelyn's curiosity sent her to see if any of the fishermen's patience had paid off with a catch of some sort.

With a level of uniformed, but assured confidence Evelyn retorted, "Ooooh, he's caught something," pointing frantically at the fishing rod of an older man wearing a tweed flatcap.

Jack leaned over behind her to examine the evidence of Evelyn's excitement.

"Evelyn that's not a fish, that's the bate!" he lovingly joked.

"OWH." The only words to leave her mouth.

The two roared with laughter as Jack teased her lovingly, wrapping her in his coat, his muscular arms sheltering her from the wind. He towered above Evelyn who's shorter height fitted perfectly into the safe place in his chest. They walked back down the pier, the air filled with a shared merriment, the edges of their mouths and their dimpled cheeks aching from the laughter. The sugary smell of seaside donuts propelled them towards the traditional ocean front stand.

Six devilish delights were placed into the white paper bag, sugar swimming, like a powdery canal at the bottom of it. They sat like an old couple in love facing the sea on a wooden bench housing a silver memorial plaque. They were at peace with one another as they slowly demolished the donuts, the ocean lapping in the distance, their lips licking with happiness.

# # #

Chapter 16

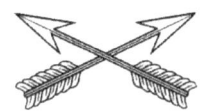

Life continued as it always did. Jack woke with the first thought to enter his mind beginning with the letter E. Evelyn smiled rolling in her heavy duvet, the sun rising as she visualized a life with Jack.

Evelyn and Jack propelled their energies into capitalizing on acting opportunities in between sharing their weekends with each other. They planned a mid-week meet up in Piccadilly circus to catch a movie. But, as they met something was off.

Evelyn immediately sensed Jack's mind was elsewhere. Their energy was no longer aligned and the excitement of seeing each other quickly subsided for the first time, quite unexpectedly upon meeting. The movie was awkward and being in the early stages of, whatever it was they were, both of them opted for a passive communication approach. The result of their silences drowning their minds in confusion. A stalemate proceeded between them as the internal tension mounted and their own stories were written. In the silence they defined their separate meanings of it as the film flickered on the screen.

Jack was distant as they sat hands apart in their cinema seats. Jack making a point of buying them separate drinks so they didn't have to share. Declining her hand as it habitual reached for him. They gazed on as the film ran. Jack left his seat abruptly upon the immediate conclusion of the film. The outside air from Leicester Square was refreshing as they exited the cinema. Jack began striding towards the station Evelyn would need to go home via, in an outwardly polite attempt to remove himself from the situation. A fast and brief hug was executed as they left each other's company.

Evelyn headed down the station steps towards the underground ticket platform, a confusion circling chaotically in her mind. Jack walked away relieved, he shouldn't have met her today with everything else that was going on.

In a moment of spontaneous thought, she made a decision. Evelyn turned on her heels. She needed an explanation for the turn of events. He always seemed to get away with not explaining to her what was going on, treating her differently when he wanted to and never being asked for an explanation as to why. Evelyn wasn't going to let this continue without an account as to why he was behaving this way today.

Brushing past the passengers coming towards her, Evelyn ran back up the underground station steps of Piccadilly Circus tube, reaching for her phone from her bag and dialing Jack's number as she went. The pavement ahead was filled with tourists.

Jack answered. "Everything ok?"

"Not really, Hun. What's going on?"

Jack's response was stern. "I don't think this is going to work. Sorry, something's not right."

"Can you come back and talk to me, please?"

"There's nothing to be said Evelyn. Go home."

A suited stranger looked on at a lost young woman. The platform was empty as he stood close by. The woman knew where she was going, but it appeared to him that she was internally lost. He watched her stepped up to the train as it pulled into the underground station, minding the gap and resting on the velvet seat next to him. The tube wheels screamed as the carriages left the station.

# # #

Weeks began to pass without a word between Jack and Evelyn as she concluded her education and followed her friend towards the financial district of the city of London as the year's contract at Finchley road came to a close. A new group of friends embarking on a glass fronted block of apartments. With her acting career just starting upon her graduation it wasn't overly important where she lived in London, just as long as she could reach the central hub easily enough for auditions. The easterly direction was ironically a lot closer to Jack's house.

They hadn't spoken, the minimal communication barely reaching the other via a handful of sporadic texts. It wasn't right between them at all. They couldn't make it happen. It was time to forget. It wasn't meant to be. The time had come to move on but, instead, time stood still.

Evelyn wiped her eyes as the financial frustration of securing acting work built up alongside her debt. She felt very alone. The fire in heart quickly losing awareness in the maze of her mind. Evelyn yearned to take back the mistake of pursuing things with Jack and return comfortably to the stability of her old relationship. Tears stained her soft young cheeks.

# # #

Chapter 17

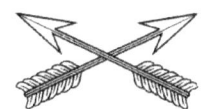

Her new apartment was beautiful. Spacious and newly built in comparison to her last place. Gazing out across the sparkling water that was warmed by the sunshine, she looked directly down contemplatively.

Thirteen floors was high, but not high enough to cause a fatality, just a mess. Anyway, she was scared of heights. Evelyn's head spun, her mind starved, her stomach screaming for a good meal. Wandering over to the cupboards she looked in hers. An old box of half-eaten, basic branded bran flakes and a cheap bottle of vodka. Hopelessly, she looked down, closing her eyes to shut it out for a brief second.

She took the vodka bottle, leaving the bran flakes to sit isolated in the bare cupboard. It wasn't that there wasn't additional food in the cupboards, there was. It belonged to her other housemates who had actually padlocked them, a war not involving Evelyn.

She had two things left. Her pride and her honesty. Two of the things, which on reflection, were probably her biggest faults.

Outside the apartment, the sun shone but Evelyn's sight was stifled, nothing looked beautiful to her anymore, not even the burning of the bright red and orange haze of the sun setting as the day drew towards a close. Her debt had mounted and in her current situation there seemed no fast way to resolve it. Although she didn't live alone, she was the loneliest she had ever been.

Evelyn sat on the sofa clutching the vodka bottle close to her chest. She had never been interested in drugs or cigarettes. Sex and alcohol were her vices. She opened the bottle and brought it to her quenching lips. Sipping and thinking. Thinking of ways out of her own mess. The migraine of problems forever circulating in a hopeless pit of survival. She continued sipping until the clear spirited liquid was slowly being drunk like a litre bottle of still water. Her taste buds numbed to the spirited taste.

Evelyn wanted to end it all. There had been too much heart ache, pain and struggle and for what? No acting work, no food and no love. Her advised educational path leading only to a trail of money to pay back. She reached for her mobile.

Dialing a saved number, a young girl with a smiling homely voice answered, familiar to Evelyn, the one sound she trusted. Trying to make sense of her slurring, the girl pleading with her to stop drinking, eventually talking her round. Tomorrow would be a new day, she kindly quoted, but the problems of today would still wake up with her.

Over tired, Evelyn took a final sip of the vodka and fell into a deep sleep, unaware that the last of the bottle was emptying on its own accord onto the wooden floor.

# # #

Jack was heading towards forty and feeling deeply depressed. He wondered how much longer would he continue with this dream and whether it would ever compound? Was he living or just existing, hoping for a miracle every day? He had pushed any woman that had ever tried to get close to him away; he had deflected the opportunities of a conventional life whilst the world around him settled, happy and content with socialized civilization. He knew there was more to life than this tiresome wait for acting work and sought to see it prevail before his eyes, his faith ever fading.

Evelyn needed a new plan. A favor was called in and she walked unwillingly to an office block for an interview. The dead end job option. There seemed to be no other way. As with most things, her childlike bouncing nature took it on the chin, it had to and so she decided if this was what God had intended, then this is what had to be done. A sickness settled in her stomach as an East End London dockyard council estate seemed to close in on her as she walked. The graffitied brick walls segregating flat roofed homes swirling in an unconnected haze, as she questioned her existence and purpose.

Covered like a well-experienced secret agent, Evelyn's exterior radiated with seemingly exuberant and positive energy and an opportunity of a position within the firm as an administrator was offered. Strolling back home, the mounting debt seemed to plateau as a way out of the black hole opened up and she was able to follow the light once more.

Enough pain for one day, Evelyn returned to a bowl of Bran Flakes and her bed to sleep off the week knowing life would change for good when the new job began the following Monday morning.

# # #

Chapter 18

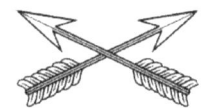

Evelyn's mobile rang by her bedside. The thought that it wouldn't be Jack prompted her to roll over and return to the more pleasant existence of her dreams than facing reality today.

When she finally encouraged herself from what had become a desolate pit of self destruction in her mind, consequently invading every cell of her body and weighing her down, Evelyn walked towards the bathroom to shower. Opening the bathroom door Evelyn half smiled at herself in the mirror, her soul willing her to pick herself up. Returning to her room she picked at a bowl of Bran Flakes once more, crisp and milk-less in the white china bowl.

Checking her phone she was surprised to see a voicemail from the acting agency she was represented by. Listening, she was even more surprised to hear the details of a television audition, which would be her first. Her laptop computer screen reiterated her lack of funds, which were highlighted within the tab of her internet banking window on the monitor.

It was amazing that she had this opportunity, but she physically had no money to fund the travel expenses to get to the audition. She rarely was able to pay to get into London, strategically planning her route to stations without ticket barriers and walking the remainder of her journeys, but this was too far. The audition was at the opposite end of the country and she would not make it there without the careful watch of at least one ticket officer. Evelyn owed her father a considerable amount of cash and squirmed at the thought of asking him for another monetary favor. But a ride was another story. That, he would agree to.

# # #

The sound of the telephone line on Evelyn's mobile phone echoed, a signal that her father had arrived to drive her to the audition. Collecting her from her apartment on the waterfront as the sun began to rise across the city, they sat side by side for the four hour journey.

Evelyn was quiet as she maintained focus for the task ahead. The street lamps flicked from on to off as the sun took over the role in illuminating the roads on their arrival into an unfamiliar city. Evelyn's father pulled into the drive leading towards the studios. Security directed him to where he could drop Evelyn off.

Kissing her father on the cheek as he wished her good luck, Evelyn walked towards the automatic doors framing the front entrance. She had never been to a television studio before. The reception looked grand as she identified a cabinet of awards the production company had won for their work.

A smiling female face greeted her as she nervously approached the front desk. The woman spoke with an accent very different from Evelyn's. Evelyn listened carefully to the woman's instructions and made her way to the casting suite with the directions she had been given.

Evelyn sat privately sweating as once more she read through her character's dialogue in the deafening silence of the jam-packed waiting room. This was the first time she had read anything for television and navigating the script was different to what she had seen laid out for theatre auditions.

Having trained exclusively in theatre, she had never stood in front of a camera before. That was, except for a yoghurt commercial, which actually just filmed her abdominal muscles as she expressed an "umm" at the creamy strawberry taste of the marketed product and didn't hear about it again.

One by one, the other actors were called into the casting suite by the assistant. In this time Evelyn maximized every second to study the sides in front of her, her pencil frantically scribbling notes to help herself on the page.

"Evelyn Wise?" a smiling assistant called her into the room. She lifted herself confidently and entered a small room, just off from where they had gathered the auditionees. A small, black portable video camera rested on a small stand, which sat next to a television monitor, before her.

With her heart racing in her chest, she began. The instance was a blur; however, she remembered that somehow, the words had flowed effortlessly. On reflection it was flawlessly memorised, which came as a surprise to

her. One by one the auditionees entered the room again.
There was a short wait after everyone had been seen, and
then, the busy assistant returned, presumably to deliver
much anticipated news.

# # #

Chapter 19

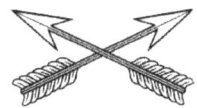

The names were called, the sound reaching Evelyn's ear in slow motion as she prayed to be included on that list. They had been informed that just three would be asked to stay behind; the rest of the auditioners would be asked to leave.

"... and Evelyn Wise.." Her heart raced with the realization that she, too would audition for them again. The room emptied as herded teenagers scuffed their feet in disappointment, a couple offering their congratulations to the three remaining candidates as they left the casting suite waiting room with their things.

Evelyn and the two other girls were called back one by one. This time, the room had a couple of new faces sitting behind a table. Unbeknownst to Evelyn, the producer had been called down to watch the recalled participants. He had already cast the role twice, but was unable to find someone who could manage the task. With the storyline set to be axed, the three women this time were the last hope on making it happen.

After reading to camera with another new scene, they were once more told to wait. The three girls were brought in together as a discussion was led detailing the demands of the role if they were to be offered it. The three young women listened carefully to the information communicated to them.

A sheer determination ran through Evelyn's bloodstream as she vowed to not leave the building without the job. After this next step only she and one other candidate remained.

The final step was to read with another actor whom they would be working with on a regular basis. Evelyn entered the room for the third time that day.

A young, male actor now stood with the casting director. "Evelyn, this is Miles. He will be reading with you today."

The boy had a beautiful air of happiness about him, his naivety and enthusiasm beaming from his cheerful smile. Evelyn read with Miles and waited patiently whilst her competitor went in after. The assistant informed them that there would be no more reading needed from them today and asked them to wait patiently for the casting director to deliver their final verdict.

The young women made idle chit chat as they waited. The girl had flaming red hair, which Evelyn admired and was chipper in their conversing. The sound of the casting director opening the door stopped Evelyn and the girl mid-conversation as they readied themselves for the decision.

The director stated that the new part was a very private affair, with an importance being stressed on the confidentiality of the storyline. Evelyn heard the news being delivered to the other girl. They began to thank her and were excited to give her a supporting part in the show.

"Evelyn?" She lifted her head. "We would like to offer you the job."

Evelyn was utterly thrilled to tell her father she wouldn't need a lift home that day.

Filming was set to begin immediately. The teams at the studio prepared Evelyn for what was to happen the next day. She was whisked around the departments of hair and makeup, costume and production before being taken back to the hotel in a taxi to rest.

Evelyn would be staying in the hotel most nights, where she would remain for six weeks until she was relocated to a place of her very own. This wasn't just a commercial, a few days here and there or an odd episode, this was a regular acting job for a minimum of six months. She was overjoyed.

# # #

Chapter 20

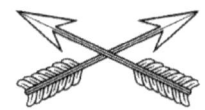

Jack was getting somewhere, but nowhere fast. He was fortunate enough to have landed a great agent and was going up for a number of small roles in television and film. He had modeled in his younger years, but after having done the theatre production at the Gielgud, he had a taste for working full time as an actor and his feet were well and truly itching.

The gym became his favourite resource for fueling his fire. Sweat leaked onto his grey t-shirt that clung to his sculpted chest as he attempted to free his mind.

The peace that returned after pushing his body to the edge of its capabilities opened up a channel for new ideas to flourish, but the sound of his cell phone put an end to it.

"I have news." The unexpected text message from Evelyn, saved under his nickname for her, made him stop for a beat. Curious, he replied.

The forthcoming messages were cryptic in her reply, but it sounded exciting and important. They had not seen each other for a few months, but that was about to change.

He arrived later with a bottle of wine as Evelyn opened the door of her apartment. It didn't take but a moment for their hearts to fill with love once again.

Their nerves were hidden under both of their naturally confident exteriors as they sat at a small, metal table on Evelyn's long balcony overlooking the water. As Jack poured the wine, the summer sun warmed them as they talked.

"So what's the news?" Jack enquired.

"I landed a part. A good one. A life changing acting opportunity Jack," Evelyn expressed.

"WOW. Go on."

Jack listened carefully to the information she relayed, his heart torn in two. He was of course happy for her. But this job would take her away. Even though he hadn't contacted her, he knew she wasn't very far, a short drive in the car, if he were to let his heart lead, and that had comforted him. Evelyn's face was lit up with happiness. Jack longed to share in her joy and hold her again.

"I leave tonight. I have already been filming. It happened so quickly, but I wanted to tell you in person," she went on.

Keeping up his heroic appearance Jack's heart sunk as she began to show him the newspaper clippings. Sitting a friendship distance apart in her packed up room on the un-slept in, made up bed, he began reading the informative articles. It was surreal.

As it had done before, time seemed to stand still as they united. The habitual longing to just hold one another over powered them both as their affections resurfaced. The centre of their palms meeting as they unconsciously reached for the other's fingertips. Their hands finally connected in the symbol of prayer as they lay next to one another innocently on the bed.

The air was filled with an energy like no other. Evelyn would leave at 9 p.m. this evening to take the four hour road trip to her permanent new home. Why was it that they were thèy always brought together just before they were about to be taken from each other? A pattern had emerged. A bold exercise in the art of letting go.

"Let me take you to dinner before you leave," Jack said. His heart warned him not to let her in too much. He shouldn't of been visiting her today, but now he didn't want to let her leave.

# # #

A stranger headed for the Royal Victoria DLR station passing a business orientated hotel with an open fronted restaurant overlooking the water of an East London dockyard. Smiling, the stranger watched a couple having a thumb war at a restaurant table. Unaware of his gaze as their laughter highlighted the best in both of them.

"Let me help you move tonight," Jack said after defeating Evelyn in their thumb war challenge. Evelyn was not expecting this suggestion but Jack's vibrant spontaneity always caught her off guard. Something she carefully disguised. His ability to excite her on the spur of the moment was one of the major reasons why she still loved him.

Although Jack had not left school with any qualifications. He was experienced with women. He had read the handbooks, more than once on how to seduce them. He knew if he helped her tonight they would make love like they use to. The best sex, like they had in the days when everyone else had work and they awaited calls from their agents for auditions. He also knew if he helped her move, her heart would stay connected to his with the distance.

Unconsciously, their love would be unpacked in her new apartment along with the rest of her belongings. He would be the first guest in her new home and her new start.

This was something Evelyn was keen not to happen. It was meant to be a new start and after everything that had happened, she had made the firm decision: Jack was not going to be in it.

Evelyn had promised a friend who also lived in London and was in the show a ride back to the studios. She was due to arrive any moment. Jack carried the last of the boxes to the car. "Evelyn's Coaches" were ready to depart, the collection of her life items pressed up against the windows of the people carrier she had borrowed for the removal operation.

Jack followed in transit. He had convinced her that his arms may come in handy when unloading at the other end and she had succumbed to the thought.

As they drove up the different motorways Evelyn and Jack zipped past each other on occasion, a fun overtaking game, and an opportunity to see the other. Another tool to be as close as possible to the other. Stopping for fuel and sweets, Evelyn and Jack locked eyes across the forecourt. Paying for her petrol, Evelyn smiled at him, her love overflowing towards him.

This would be a smile that would stay with him forever. The sun was beginning to rise as Evelyn dropped her fellow cast member home before continuing on to her new place with Jack in convoy.

# # #

Chapter 21

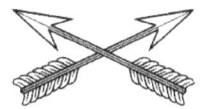

Jack scrawled the words on a piece of cardboard that had been left in his car, the remains of a pizza box.

UNLOADING ROYAL KEY
UNLOADING ROYAL QUAY

Evelyn watched on smiling as Jack struggled over the spellings for his make shift sign so his car wouldn't get clamped and potentially towed away from being illegally present in the apartment block car park.

Even though they should be exhausted after driving through the night, on arrival they playfully improvised imaginary scenarios on why they were transporting the boxes and what they could have been delivering, experimenting with differing emotions for acting practice, naturally.

The cars were unpacked and whilst showering Evelyn realised she had not yet purchased any bath towels. Discovering this too late, Jack and Evelyn playfully dried themselves off using their clothes, before collapsing on the clean white bedding, gently kissing.

With care, Jack's strong hands held Evelyn's petite waist and their passion for each other was reignited. As the moment began to heat up, rolling over their aroused clothed lower regions pressed firmly together and the wooden slats under the heavenly mattress gave way. Laughing as Jack, shocked, fell through the gap onto the floor. With animalistic movements, he picked his young beauty back up; Her feminine laughter was cancelled out by his kiss. They had broke the bed on the first night.

It was early and the red sky marked the beginning of a new dawn. After a short nap Evelyn and Jack made love again before walking upstairs to fetch a glass of water unclothed. They lay peacefully, naked, talking, stretched out on both sides of the L shaped sofa of the upside down penthouse.

Their conversations took them to another universe, two souls raw and open, revealing themselves fully in the safety of the other's company. The red dawn radiated through the windows as the world slept and the freer spirits that remained awake in the early hours were able to live out and speak their truths. The two bedrooms downstairs were separated by a stylishly designed white wooden staircase that led to the separate lounge and dining room space upstairs, complete with a small galley kitchen and another minimalistic bathroom.

The apartment was very modern, white washed and massively minimalist. It was on the top floor of the apartment block and like her last London apartment, it was also by the water and glass fronted. Napping in each others arms, their soft words faded as they fell back into a satisfying sleep.

Upon waking, the couple showered and exited the apartment in search of food. They walked around the fresh and modern dockland complex, deciding on a Starbucks coffee in a rather unusual music memorabilia museum. Pictures of the Beetles and other musicians were framed on the colorful walls which the two of them observed as they sipped their hot drinks.

Jack packed up his things when they returned from their coffee; Evelyn wanted him to stay and live there with her, not that she would ever ask him to. He kissed her gently goodbye as she closed the door and he waited in the lobby for the lift. Standing patiently he smiled, looking back at the door. He drove home with a heart full of love.

# # #

Chapter 22

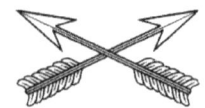

To celebrate her recent acting success, Evelyn planned a party back home at her London flat. She loved being a host and whenever the chance arose she often got a group together and it usually had a theme.

Before tonight it had been a Hawaiian night, complete with a sandpit and a limbo competition with the guests in hula skirts and Caribbean style shorts and shirts. Her kind housemates blew up balloons and the TV screen was placed centre stage.

Evelyn's first episode of the new television series she was starring in would be shared with all her closest friends. All the people who had shared in her struggle were now sharing in her success. Evelyn was filming all day. On the day of the party, she grabbed a taxi from the studios and headed for the station. The party was set to start at seven this evening and guests were already arriving.

The alcohol was flowing. Evelyn's housemates had laid out bowls of crisps and tasty treats in front of a selection of spirits the guests were invited to share. The speakers sat proudly either side of the main living room where the perfected playlist could be heard throughout the apartment including the balcony, their designated smoking area. The Greenwich Millennium dome glowed as the water below glistened in the moonlight.

The train journey from Evelyn's new apartment down to the party would take just over two hours. Freshening up, very unglamorously in the carriage toilet cubicle, Evelyn was really excited to be returning to the familiarity of her old life. So much had changed in such a short period of time, for the better of course, but the extensive amount of adapting had exhausted her.

Evelyn finished touching up her make up. Sipping some bottled water she positively enjoyed a break from her usual intellectual reads to indulge fully in a trashy magazine. The conductor of the train announced the final stop of today's journey and the sixteen coaches slowly drew themselves towards the platform at Euston train station.

# # #

Jack King sat restlessly in his car watching his phone. He had arranged to pick Evelyn up from the station and would be her date for the party.

It had been a number of weeks since he had helped her move. He was overly confident with most women, but Evelyn gave him butterflies. She beamed at him as he got out of the car to greet the traveling gypsy, her fun energy radiating. Jack took her bag and placed it into the back seat of the car. Once seated in the passenger side, Evelyn planted a soft thank you kiss on his cheek; Jack returning the sweet gesture unconsciously with one on her forehead. They locked hands, fingers entwined, reconnected again.

He whizzed through King Cross and back out towards the East End of London, returning his right hand to hers in between changing gears in the manual car. They would be fashionably late. The enjoyable conversation ran in parallel with the attraction they felt for one another, a friendship most couples would be envious of.

Evelyn had a number of admirers at the party, old flames were amongst the grand mix of people she had come to know living in London but no one at that party held her heart like Jack did and she was excited to finally introduce him to her friends.

They could hear the music playing from the apartment as they parked opposite the water's edge. A couple of friends smoking off the long width of the balcony noticed Jack and Evelyn arrive and called the news to the others inside.

Jack carried Evelyn's bag over his shoulder, taking her hand as they climbed the steps up to the apartment entrance. Entering the lift they kissed passionately in an attempt to maximise this private moment before they entered the party.

Pushing the front door open they placed Evelyn's smart black weekend suitcase in her old room that was located immediately ahead of them as they entered the apartment. The room was now ladened with guests' coats and sleeping bags, evidence that they were to enter a good turn out.

Jack charmed her friends as Evelyn enjoyed having everyone she loved in one place. Jack and Evelyn frequently caught each other's eyes across the crowd.

After the introductions had been made, they rejoined each other and settled on the balcony together. Finding their own corner to nestle in, looking out over the water, Jack's arm was wrapped around Evelyn's. She leant her head into the perfect place on his chest as they talked. They had never placed any label on what they were, the distance and their careers making excuses for both of them, finding it difficult to fully commit to one another. With her fearlessness and a couple of glasses of wine, Evelyn raised her concern about other women to Jack. Their hearts opened, him equally raising his concerns about other men and her being in a show with a group of extremely handsome younger male actors.

"There are no other women trust me. The only thing you have to worry about is me getting caught and going to prison and that is not going to happen, believe me."

He kissed her gently on the forehead embracing her. For Evelyn there was no safer place than in the arms of Jack's protection. Interrupting the moment, Evelyn's housemate and fellow host stumbled out, having had a few too many to drink, and began snapping away with her camera at the unofficial couple with a coo of aww's. Jack and Evelyn joined the rest of the party on the makeshift dance floor, Jack twirling her around as her friends looked on.

After the a few fun tracks changed, Evelyn spun happily over to an old friend who was smiling at her.

"He is no good for you Evelyn, are you seeing him?" the man protested.

"Well yes, kind of, sort of, it's complicated. Why?"

"Stay away from him Evelyn," the man replied sternly.

"Why are you saying this to me? I thought you would be happy for me."

"I am, but just trust me." He had had a couple of beers, but still Evelyn was rattled. What was he talking about? She knew they knew of each other.

"He is seeing someone else," the man revealed.

"What?" Evelyn turned back, in shock at what she had just heard. The jubilant night turning quickly sour.

"Last time I saw him, he never mentioned your name, he mentioned someone else's."

Evelyn took herself away from the main party area along the corridor to her room to think. Her head was buzzing. She knew the men had encountered each other a long time ago. The comment could have possibly been made before Evelyn had met Jack, but she wasn't sure.

Jack stood watching the man who had just been talking to Evelyn. He sensed something was up. He also sensed this man might have a soft spot for Evelyn.

Jack was just over six foot, broad, and muscular; he had been around the block. He approached the man Evelyn had just walked away from.

Harry Red was a bald, older man, an ex marine and also an actor. He and Jack had worked on a commercial together, Jack's boastful comments now backfiring on him.

"Alright mate?" Jack smiled

"Not bad, thank you, Jack. How are you?" Harry puffed up his chest to disguise his nervousness at the situation and Jack's intimidation.

"So what were you and Evelyn discussing? She didn't look too happy." Jack asked charmingly, testing the waters.

"Nothing in particular; you know, this and that. How are you?" Harry steered the conversation in a new direction.

"Very well, Harry, very well, mate. Well good to see you." The men shook hands with burning hatred.

"Look after yourself," Jack said patronizingly winking and then smirking at him as he left. Harry's chest deflated as Jack left the room to find Evelyn.

Jack found Evelyn with a group of her friends in her room and stood in the doorway smiling at her, encouraging her to come and talk to him. She hadn't said anything to them; she just wanted to escape her own thoughts by joining in their merriment whilst she put off thinking about what Harry had just said. They went quietly into one of the empty bedrooms to talk as Evelyn retold Harry's story to Jack.

"Evelyn he fancies you. He is going to say what he can to get you away from me. I met him ages ago and what he is talking about...this was all before I met you."

Evelyn was confused. The alcohol disrupting her usually clear mind. She loved Jack. She had not seen Harry for a long time, although he was there for her when Jack decided to ignore her, telling her that she was too young and it wasn't going to work. A reoccurring theme of there on/off relationship that fueled Evelyn with frustration.

She was torn. They looked at each other. Hearts pumping, they didn't want to end this or have someone spoil this perfect evening. Evelyn knew Harry liked her. He had said so on a number of occasions; tonight she would give Jack the benefit of the doubt.

# # #

Chapter 23

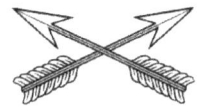

That night they slept in his bed downstairs at Jack's. It looked like he was going to employ his illegal upstairs expansion idea, much to Evelyn's disappointment, which she kept to her self. Jack was angry at Harry and even after Evelyn's insistence not to, he phoned Harry to put him straight.

Jack drove Evelyn the two hours from his house to Euston Station letting her go once more the following day. Kissing him goodbye and rolling her suitcase across the station towards the platform.

Driving back, Jack thought fondly of the weekend resisting his needy feelings of not knowing when he would see her again. He didn't know what this was, how he really felt; he resisted falling for this free spirit who would undoubtedly break his heart.

Traveling back they each reflected happily on their feelings for the other. A warm glow in their hearts, accompanying the separate coffees they each purchased for their returns to routine.

# # #

The next weekend arrived quickly as Evelyn turned off the motorway and headed towards the seaside. Jack sat on the sofa relaxed and sensed her drawing closer. It was almost like they were beyond conventional communication at times. A sixth sense, a burning glow in his chest, navigating her through a sensual satellite system.

Without discussing with Evelyn who had travelled the long distance alone, the radio for company, content at reaching her destination which felt like home in her heart, Jack walked confidently out of his house and up to the main road to wait on the pavement with a smile as she drove up it.

Parking in front of his house and tired from driving, she resisted the thousands of fun kisses he planted on her as she opened her car door, secretly loving every one of them. The sky was clear as Jack retrieved her things from the car boot. Placing them by the side of the car, Jack held Evelyn closely as both of them looked up at the starlit illuminated sky. A shooting star crossed the atmosphere as they looked into each other's eyes. The inner peace overflowing inside of them.

Evelyn's heart sunk as he turned. A black bruise coated his right eye. Smiling as if it wasn't there, Jack picked Evelyn up swinging her around, glad she was back. Entering the house he swiftly carried her up the stairs, kissing her as they went.

# # #

A sharp blade now glistened in the morning sunlight, which Jack had tied to the right hand side of the bed as

Evelyn's beautiful brown eyes gazed at it, laying surrendered in the sheets entwined with Jack. The symbol of this weapon identified to Evelyn that his situation had worsened a great deal.

She wanted to help him desperately but was scared to ask him what she could do in case he rejected her again. She wouldn't question it now; he was happy and wasn't worrying about his problems in this instance. The moment was precious. Unbeknown to them at the time. Unforgettable.

A fierce muscular Pitbull dog barked downstairs, jealous his owner's attention had been taken by Evelyn's visit. Tending to the dog, Jack rolled off Evelyn who watched as his firm naked legs wandered out of the room.

She lay looking around the empty space. Her mind notifying her that he was too old for her. What would happen in ten, twenty, thirty years from now? This would be a fleeting affair; they both knew it deep down but the power of this lust surely meant more, the fate of their meeting, the passion between them.

Evelyn set the thoughts to one side. The only thing she had was this moment and this is what she would focus on.

Jack pottered in his spacious kitchen, now comfortably dressed and carefully preparing two bowls of porridge. He liked having Evelyn stay. Life meant something when he knew she was lying safely in his bed. The sun shone through his kitchen window. A beautiful feeling of peace settled in him as he watched his trusty canine companion worn out from his jealousy and now snoring by the sofa. He called up to Evelyn that her breakfast was ready. They played house, even if it was for five minutes, they lived there together.

Striding down the stairs in his baggy t-shirt, she hugged him from behind, her figure connecting to his like the chinese symbol of yin yang.

"What's this?" Jack uttered.

"A backwards cuddle." Evelyn smiled.

Both dressed, Jack dug out a pair of old wellington boots in a smaller size to what he wore and explained to Evelyn that they belonged to his niece. They both knew they belonged to another woman, most probably Jack's ex who he shared the house with before.

Holding Evelyn's delicate hand, Jack always thought it felt right. It fitted his perfectly. He was a man on a mission, strong in his strides as they walked hand in hand across the grassy marshland and out towards the sea, the dog running contentedly up ahead.

The open space didn't often occupy many visitors so their consciousness of the age gap was gratefully undisturbed. The sea calmed everything. They were both on such personal journeys, at very different stages in their individual pathways but for a moment, a harmony, a stillness, a feeling of completeness resided in their happy silence.

Towards the return part of their walk stood a huge white house, complete with tennis courts the opposite side of the gravel track. The perfect family home. Silently they both imagined having this home together. As the walks began to become more familiar they discussed this shared thought. Building room by room in their imaginations, laughing at the absurdity of their ideas.

Of course there would be a rock climbing wall up one side of it and a swimming pool for the kids and space for all their A List friends to park their luxurious cars for the extravagant parties they would host as a couple.

# # #

Evelyn sat casually with the lid closed on the toilet later that afternoon, talking to Jack whilst he lay outstretched in the bath full of white bubbles. The steam rising off the recently run, hot bath. His skin was always soft but with his age and training it was thinner than that of her ex boyfriends.

It was never in her plan to love Jack. Not this much. She playfully convinced him to try applying a face mask as he watched her meticulously brush her teeth. She began cementing the green plaster around her own face until only her beautiful brown eyes radiated from under the hardening green texture. He looked on, watching her innocence, the load on his mind lifting, a peaceful smile creeping from his lips as he agreed with embarrassment to join in with the face mask fun. Jack's dog pushed the door open with his nose, took one look at Jack's face and wandered back out, which made them both chuckle.

Evelyn perched on the bath edge, and together, they looked ridiculous. She leant in to him, a comedic like kiss was strategically shared, avoiding the green plaster on their faces from touching.

Although she came across strong, Evelyn's frame was tiny. A size 6, toned with a bum that men desired. A lot. Jack was addicted to satisfying her. He had been with many women, but sex with Evelyn was unlike anything he had experienced before.

It was odd each time Evelyn left, a stale silence emerged between the two of them. Text messages not replied to. Communication stopped. A frustration followed by a confused state of mind on both parts, exiting the easiest way they knew how, passively walking away. The unexplained was left to fester as clustering tension locked in their bodies.

Jack knew what to say to brainwash her. His ego loved the attention of women. The more he could manipulate them, the more powerful he felt. Evelyn dug her heels in. She might love him, but this love could quickly turn to loathing as she began to realize the trap she had become a part of.

# # #

Chapter 24

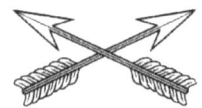

Evelyn had been asked to return to London for two interviews to talk about her new acting role. The publicity department arranging transport and a very nice hotel in central London, overlooking the iconic sights of Big Ben and The Millennium Wheel on the Embankment of the River Thames.

Work was a priority as was the need to focus fully on the professional task at hand. But her mind wandered and her desire to share such an experience with her soul mates beckoned. Evelyn called in her friends, who were excited to party and see her new fashionable designer outfits she would wear for the interviews.

They purchased some wine on the way, dropping into her hotel room after work, looking forward to seeing their best friend since she had moved away from London for her new acting job.

Evelyn was ecstatic, and excited to see them, buzzing from the highs of this new career adventure. Her radio interview played through the speakers on the hotel plasma television screen as the girls listened in, like teenagers awaiting the arrival of a heartthrob. The girls happily hugging Evelyn as her unique voice resonated through the speakers, overly proud of their friend's achievements.

Evelyn brought a video camera for the occasion to document the achievement on camera. Happily, she whizzed it around the room describing her good fortune and documenting her wealth of happiness in this moment.

As the evening progressed, her friends headed home, work beckoning them the next morning as they began finishing up the remainder of their wine left in their glasses. A strong knock came at the hotel room door as Evelyn opened it with a romantic anticipation. She had not seen him in a suit since she had watched him in his show, never in person. The sharp black jacket rested on his broad shoulders, a white collar gleaming around the outline of his upper chest, top button undone, a black tie loose around his neck, like an overly persuasive aftershave advert. Jack stood with a bottle of red wine and squeezed Evelyn's hand reassuringly as he walked in, introducing himself to her friends.

Leaving them alone, Evelyn's friends said their goodbyes to her and Jack. Their girlie chit chat echoing down the expensively decorated hotel corridor as they went. Jack gazed lovingly at Evelyn, a sense of peace silencing his mind. Evelyn yearned to hear his thoughts out loud as the hot red summer sun began to lower in the smokey London skyline. Making their way to the window they silently looked out across the city as Jack typically spotted a couple wearing very little with no sign of any curtains as they began to get closer.

His excitement was like a child at Christmas, increasing as Evelyn notified him of the ability to zoom in on her hand held video camera as they both watched closely to the live "pants party" across from them. They laughed as it ended without any action, Jack now standing at ease behind Evelyn as they looked out of the glass fronted bedroom, the sun setting on the city.

Sensually his lips met the back of her neck in the silence. Kissing her until she weakened and the ecstasy continued until she eventually turned around resting her hands on his chest passionately kissing him in return. His hand slid inside the side of her dress, climbing up towards her braless, hard, young breasts squeezing them before racing his hand towards her crotch firmly. His black suit jacket was casually thrown onto the poised puffy pillowcases of the double hotel bed. Picking her up, Evelyn wrapped her bare legs around his waist as he pressed the back of her hoisted smart black dress up against the glass, the only surface between them and the twenty-three floors below. Evelyn slowly undid the rest of the buttons on Jack's shirt, kissing down his toned bare chest as he crossed towards the bed and lay her down.

# # #

Jack walked naked into the black minimalist marble bathroom, drawing a bath for two. The steam rising from the bubbles as he and Evelyn dipped their toes and then relaxed into the warm water, which swirled between them as they gazed lovingly into the depths of one another's souls from opposite ends of the tub.

Pearls of crystalised water droplets clung as they stepped out of the water and huge white towel robes hugged their naked bodies. As they warmed themselves in the cozy room, thoughts of food were now prominent in their ravenous minds.

Jack moved to the lounge area of the hotel suite scanning the chic room service menu as Evelyn's fresh feet were comforted by the complimentary hotel slippers. Cuddled up, the order was placed and they decided on a movie to watch while they waited, hands wandering as the credits rolled. The fire between them was fanned out by the delivery of dinner at the door.

A sparkling silver chrome trolley topped with a bright, white plain tablecloth was wheeled into the suite by a smart suited doorman. A platter of indulgent and edible treats were disguised by the shining silver lids they were housed under. Their appetites were ravenous from their amorous workout as they tucked in immediately, napkins laid across their laps. As the evening went on, Evelyn turned her attention to the morning interviews ahead. Jack gathered his things and began to leave in anticipation. The struggle between them always arose at this point as Evelyn questioned why he never stayed the night, her mind circulating into a frenzy of possibilities.

Jack, unaware of her doubting demeanor, lived a long drive from Central London and was keen to start his daily routine from home and avoid the discombobulating effects of the populous city rush hour. A passive aggression began to boil as their conflicting internal discussions leaked their way to the surface and a stalemate silence prevailed in their bittersweet goodbye.

They lay awake in their separate beds, eyes wide, staring at the same moon, their hearts questioning the confusion of their feelings.

# # #

Jack sat with his coffee at home as Evelyn's live interview was due to air. The camera crew quickly reestablishing themselves to another area of the studio floor as they broke for commercials. Evelyn was thrust into a chair as a countdown began.

"3,2,1 and were LIVE!" The presenters smiles widened as Evelyn composed herself in her surreal surroundings. The studio was awash with bright painted colours and a plasma screen now showing a large picture of Evelyn's face as she answered a short firing of interview questions.

Jack smiled at the screen while watching Evelyn, and finding it hard to fathom that this was the woman he had made love to just last night. A jealously of some sort slopped in his stomach. He didn't think he was envious, but in some strange way he was.

He did love her, he knew that. He knew he craved her, but like Evelyn, work would come first. It had too. The discipline of actors is much like that of any other, skills must be maintained, developed and practiced. Focus, concentration and a sheer determination on the goal in sight must never waiver. Someone would have to give; both would have to make this relationship a priority, if they wanted this just as much. They could have both but they would have to know it was possible to achieve. A beautiful relationship and outstanding acting careers, the fate of the outcome was in their beliefs.

A unknown number rung on Jack's phone as he answered curiously. A cash in hand calling, beckoned him. The man on the line spoke sternly, relaying a meeting spot on the way to the job, which was unidentified in detail in case the call was traced. Jack agreed and hung up the phone as he sat back in the comfort of his sofa staring blankly ahead. He hadn't dreamt of his life like this. His wild imagination had invented plans of genius. He had hoped to be a superman amongst other men. The fight to get there, however, was never expected to be this painful. The average man's normalcy, a routine he once detested, now had an enlightening appeal.

Jack rested his hands behind his head as his dog sat faithfully by his side. Behind the mounting debt, chaos and unplanned path he was walking, he smiled. The riches Jack possessed lay in his hope, a wealth and fortune buried deep within his soul that no man could take from him whilst it continued to burn brightly. The job drew closer and survival kicked in.

# # #

Chapter 25

Evelyn had been invited to an event at The British Academy of Film and Television Awards (BAFTA) by a friend. It was an enjoyable networking opportunity and another chance to visit the city of London. The shiny black taxi raced through the back streets avoiding the rush hour traffic, its wheels enjoying the puddles poised in the potholes. Jack was informed she would be in town and offered to meet her and take her out for drinks and dinner afterwards.

The large, gleaming gold iconic BAFTA mask greeted Evelyn and her two guests as they were signed in by a finely dressed woman at the front desk. Once through the doors, the networking hive of chatter and group mingling welcomed them. They headed to the bar, a comfort zone to nestle in, before stepping out into the unknown selection of strangers.

Evelyn radiated energy and took to the event with ease, introducing herself and her guests to suited directors and other industry professionals as silver trays of exquisite nibbles, circulated at mouth height by the smartly dressed catering staff.

Matted business cards exchanged friendly hands and were sealed with firm hand shakes as new faces were greeted with a smile. Interest arose as the curiosity to find out what the next person did prevailed through the introductions.

Jack parked in his favorite spot and made his way down Shaftesbury Avenue across Piccadilly circus and on to BAFTA to meet Evelyn. The address at 195 Piccadilly warmly welcomed him, its doors headed with the familiar logo. Energized, he smiled sweetly at the front desk, as he assured them he was just meeting a friend and would not be staying long.

Evelyn spotted him immediately from the conversation she was engaged in. His tall appearance made him easily distinguishable from the crowd. He greeted Evelyn with a kiss on the cheek as she proudly introduced him to her guests above the increasingly loud background chatter. Evelyn's guests decided to stay on for a little while longer as Jack's hand connected once again with Evelyn's, leading his lady towards the exit. A stranger on the street looked on as the happy couple swung their held hands high like infant school children in love.

The bright lights of Piccadilly Circus soon bathed them in an electronic wash of red and orange flashes as digitalized advertisements took their turns to announce their information to the Saturday night city goers. Jack was keen to introduce Evelyn to a friend of his, who was enjoying a colourful cocktail in a gay bar across from the infamous Gielgud Theatre Stage Door.

Jean Pierre was stereotypical of the type of men who drank in this particular bar. His extroverted feminine persona instantly activated on Jack's arrival as he sipped his rainbow fizzing drink through a thin pink straw with pursed lips. Jean Pierre was a hairdresser in London and had cut Jack's hair for a number of years. His outspoken, yet fun jealously toward Evelyn mirrored his obvious attraction to Jack. Jack could not remember the last time he had paid for a hair cut.

Jean Pierre's gay friends gathered around to study Jack, showering him with compliments, constructing the changes they would implement if they were to date him, as Jack, slightly embarrassed but enjoying the ego rub, waded through the collection of gay men to the bar. Evelyn smiled on in the merriment watching Jack's handling of the situation in amusement. Arriving at the bar he kissed her gently on the forehead and ordered their drinks, giving her a cuddle as the good looking barman shook the cocktail shaker.

Evelyn sipped her sharp Mojito as Jean Pierre casually quizzed her. Jack had previously confided in him, telling him in detail of his fondness for Evelyn. As she sat with his friends, Jack began to realise just how much he was falling in love with her.

Evelyn's eyes darted from one friend to another as Jack watched her discuss her current acting responsibilities with the overtly expressive men. The cocktail straw's dry suction announced the end of Evelyn's iced rum and mint drink. The mint leaves left lying on the remnants of the crushed ice at the bottom of the glass.

"Get her home!" Jean Pierre playfully expressed. "What I would do if I were you Evelyn!"

Winking in Jack's direction, Jean Pierre said his goodbyes to the couple as they headed out of the ultra violet and pink bar, which was aptly located opposite the Gielgud theatre stage door, where Evelyn and Jack had first met. They walked together through the back streets of Soho entertained by the Saturday night sights.

People spilled out onto the road from the pavements as nightclubs, bars and theatres delivered people outside. Jack held open the door as Evelyn headed towards the two tall empty red stalls left at the bar of a beautiful hotel.

They ordered their next drinks smiling at each other. Neither of them were the soppy type but in each other's company they often couldn't help themselves. The conversation between them flowed freely and inevitably led to a discussion about their dream lives and the ideal place they would live in together. In their world, they were limitless.

Evelyn's phoned accessed the internet as they looked through pictures of the finest apartments available. Tweaking the designs with comments of what they might do, expressing the fun they would have living there and their new daily routines.

Jack gnawed at some appetizers that were served to him at the bar; Evelyn was full from divulging from the trays of nibbles earlier in the evening. With the world of realism lost, the whirlwind of their romance became caught up in the fun fantasies the future could have in store for them. They were both enjoying the alcohol piercing their veins.

After returning from the bathroom, Jack told Evelyn that there was something he wanted to show her downstairs. He settled the bill and the now slightly tipsy couple were on the move. On the way down the stairs to the lower ground floor of the hotel Evelyn passed a huge vase of beautifully tall purple flowers. As they reached the bottom Jack pulled open a heavy and grand looking door. Following him inside, a huge secret screening room revealed itself. It was like a sacred treasure chest and the fact that they weren't suppose to be in there only added to the magic and alcoholic adventure.

It smelt brand new as they walked up and back along the seated aisles, the black blank screen offering up endless imaginative opportunities for their minds to invent the possibilities of them starring on the screen. Jack sat back visualizing himself on the screens in one of the red cinema style chairs and called Evelyn over to sit with him.

The silence of the black and red screening room isolated their love, a snapshot in time, snuggled in the saintlike red seats. The innocence of their hopes resting in the home of their dreams. As they exited the screening room discreetly, Jack planted a kiss on Evelyn's forehead whilst another vase of tall stemmed violet Allium Giganteum flowers attracted Evelyn's gaze. In her cheeky mint mojito mood, she gave in to her urge to have one, plucking it from the vase as macho Jack became anxious they would get caught. She insisted she needed it and walking side by side they hid the stolen flower between them, leaving the hotel like a comedy duo.

Happy with flower in hand, Evelyn held onto Jack's muscular arm with the other, as they strolled down the cobblestoned street to a late night diner for a coffee. On their arrival the owner of the arty diner welcomed them inside. Film soundtrack music played from the speakers as the steam iron of the coffee machine hissed happily. Jack ordered an expresso whilst Evelyn opted for a soya mocha.

The diner was sparse and had no tables, but housed high stalls along a ledge the width of the wall where pictures of movie stars hung, a snug habitat of a film collector.

Evelyn enjoyed the music dancing inside the cafe to the universally recognized tunes as Jack watched on smiling. A kind, old man in a dull, sand coloured flatcap, wearing fingerless gloves looked over, a smile leaving his weathered face as he became revived by Evelyn's enthusiasm. A european couple kissed over an ice cream in the corner, the night life drawing to a close. Evelyn and Jack finished their coffee's, walking towards the Embankment.

The hotel was a fair stroll from where they were now. As they reached the location of Seven Dials they stopped, a chalk drawing up ahead, catching their attention on the pavement. A street artist had sketched a brightly colored spectacle on the grey concrete. The traditional, black street lights filled the area with a white glow illuminating the positive piece of art. A pastel shaded white dove sat with one wing, fully spread, on the top left hand side of a large red and blue painted heart. On it the artist had penned the words 'All you need is love' written delicately with bold precision inside the shape. Evelyn lay her flower down, relieving her hand of it as they both contemplated the image in separate silences. They wandered contemplatively on.

It was nearly two o'clock in the morning and the walking had slowed to a snail's pace, the timelessness continuing as the romantic evening setting reached a climatic peak on the Waterloo bridge.

To the left the business district, to the right the houses of Parliament and the famous clock tower of Big Ben. The National Theatre danced in differing colors and upon realizing her hands were now holding a pair of heels, Evelyn questioned, "Where's my flower?" A shoeless Evelyn pondered thoughtfully around her own dilemma.

Jack smiled knowingly as they walked back over the water for the final part of their evening journey to the hotel. The dark waters of the Thames River lapped up the sides of the embankment. A city divided by its powerful current. Lights from the impressive architectural historic buildings decorated the romantic landscape of this night's sky as the lost purple flowered head of Allium Giganteum lay still. The fresh, long green stem, was positioned horizontally, underlining the words of the chalk picture on the pavement--All you need is love.

Jack grabbed Evelyn as soon as the hotel suite door opened. Furiously kissing her as she weakened to his persuasive touch. They couldn't help themselves around each other as their overwhelming desire to satisfy took over. Jack held her closely, sweat clinging to his toned abs. Evelyn rested her hand on his face, kissing him passionately. Their passion continued into the night as the world watched. The extraordinary view of the romantic city sights offering the couple a perfect view opposite the bed through the front glass wall.

It was late morning as Evelyn awoke, a spare space next to her in the bed. Jack wasn't in the room. Climbing out of the hotel suite bed a knock came at the hotel room door. Checking her face in the mirror she covered herself in a hotel robe and peaked through the spy hole. Jack smiled sweetly carrying a plastic shopping bag.

"Did you think I wouldn't come back?" he questioned.

Evelyn sighed with a grin. "I hope you brought me some breakfast," she replied, pretending to be unimpressed.

He emptied the bag on the bed. Two bananas and two tubs of Oats So Simple porridge pots. They just needed to add water. Sitting on the bed using the complimentary hotel coffee and teaspoons, they looked out over the city. The sun was shining peacefully as they consumed the contents of their porridge contentedly.

# # #

Chapter 26

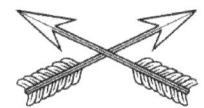

They made their way back to Jack's home by the sea. Jack helped Evelyn down as they climbed the rocks behind the wooden barrier to reach the sand. Jack's dog's excitement to get to the water was evident in his hurry to navigate his four legs down the piled stones, skidding as he bounded to the sand. Jack held her hand as she crossed the last few rocks and jumped down onto the soft English seaside sand.

He kissed her in the silence; there was no one else in sight for miles as the coastline offered a private place of peace. Jack watched as Evelyn chased his dog playfully, kicking off her shoes with a childlike innocence and then rolling up her jeans as she paddled in the water. From his bag, Jack pulled out a throw away camera, keen to capture the moment. He sat on his jacket on the rocks calling to Evelyn who ran back up the beach towards him with the dog barking in tow. She smiled embarrassed at his attempt to take a close up of her with the plastic camera purchased from Boots.

From his bag he also pulled a thin book. The book contained scenes written by modern playwrights including a selection of duologues. Sitting side by side they enthusiastically discussed a handful of suitable reads. With one firm arm around Evelyn to shield her from the wind, Jack's other hand held the edge of the book and they began.

The words were spoken eloquently from the page, the two of them enjoying the opportunity to read the dialogue of their own assigned characters from the exerts together. Their internal excitement for anything to do with acting always united them. They shared the same love. A love that only another passionate actor could understand. The wind blew around them as the plays were brought to life from the pages of the book on the sea shore. She giggled as he tried out accents. His sore ego leading to a play fight on the sand as Evelyn's wriggling was cemented with a kiss from Jack on the solitary shore. The dog began barking in circles around them as they laughed exhaustedly from the quick burst of unexpected exercise.

Later on that evening as they readied themselves for rest, Jack pulled the plug on the bath as Evelyn lay with a book on the bed. With the sea salt scrub washed off his muscular body, he wrapped himself up in a large white fluffy towel. Tiptoeing across the exposed floorboards towards the bedroom he peaked in. Noticing Evelyn wasn't looking he jumped on her playfully, his dripping wet hair flicking on Evelyn's face as she laughed.

His sister's wedding was nearing and Jack, although enjoying Evelyn's company decided he needed to go alone. He would wait until she had gone, it would be less stressful than telling Evelyn his altered decision face to face. On receiving this wholly confusing signal after another enjoyable weekend, Evelyn decided enough was enough and no reply to this remark would reach his phone.

The confusing lack of communication created a wall of stubborn silence between them. One night as Jack sat restlessly on the sofa, he flicked through the channels and saw her face smiling back at him from the TV show she starred in. The television was zapped off by his fingers on the remote. He promised himself to focus.

"NO MORE, JACK!" He reaffirmed to himself in his mind. He would move on. With another woman in his sights he would train his mind to stop thinking of Evelyn.

He caressed a new love's fair skin. His eyes closed willing himself to focus on this new relationship. They had met on a new acting job, his charms invigorating her darker side, their flirting on set leading to a burning desire to take it further. He pulled her top over her long hair, pushing her up against the hotel room wall, their adjoining rooms making the chemistry and temptation too much to resist. They crashed into the pristine white tiled bathroom as she freed his belt quickly out of its buckle.

# # #

It was Evelyn's day off from filming. A day for fitness and the treadmill was going to get a run for its money. She loved to run. As a child she had never seen a reason to walk when you could get there faster by running. Usually she would get pumped up by the perfect playlist, but today she opted for the odd occasion to watch the television on the flat screens up ahead. Fitness relieved her busy mind, an escape from the world. A group of women laughed on a day time chat show on one of the screens, another had the football highlights and directly in front of Evelyn, commercials played awaiting the start of another daytime show.

One commercial played in particular. It was almost unreal. Jack Wise shirtless, yet completely out of reach. He was the face of the next commercial playing. Evelyn's feet now felt every step from the electrical rolling treadmill track underneath her. Time slowed down to slow motion for those brief few seconds. The rest of the gym was completely unaware of her briefly unstable world.

Her legs turned to jelly as she made her way to the changing rooms quieting her mind's idle chatter. The temptation to contact him played incessantly on her mind for the next two days as she decided firmly against it.

A tall, fair haired man waited in the script department as Evelyn came in casually to collect her new scripts that had been left in her tray. She opened it to find a cheeky handwritten note penned by the middle aged man. The man in the same department that now waited. Evelyn was unaware of his lusting gaze. In the corner of the production office a group of script supervisors gathered with a director who caught Evelyn's eye. Upon seeing that she had received his note in a wholly professional manner for the rest of the groups benefit, he called her over.

The group discussed matters of importance. The main emphasis of it being placed on a scene requiring a small stunt the following day. Evelyn felt in her pocket for the note left in her tray as she listened amused to the director who had written it minutes before. She was instructed to take the elevator instead of the stairs today. The lift doors closed. They were the only ones inside the only private space away from prying eyes.

The sexual tension on set had been increasing for weeks. The tall handsomely rugged looking man grabbed Evelyn, kissing her with urgency. She gave in to the touch of his lips on her neck enjoying the spontaneous action as he released her just before the lift doors opened. An unexpected executive producer greeted them both pleasantly as the doors opened and they innocently walked out. The director from the lift walked Evelyn to her car. The resemblance from a scene in the show they had been shooting was uncanny, but for that moment entertaining.

A few months passed and both Jack and Evelyn were successful in putting their feelings and thoughts for the other to the back of their mind, experimenting with the idea of being with other people.

Evelyn was set to star in a spin off show. The majority of scenes requiring a heavy schedule of night shoots. She was called to make-up in the afternoon where she and the crew would film from four in the afternoon until four in the morning. She was in her element as the camera men laid the track for the next shot.

As she returned to her dressing room for a costume change, she smiled feeling grateful to be doing what she loved every day. The third assistant directors radio requested for her to be back on set. With a spring in her step she happily obliged.

# # #

Jack was excited as he flew off to film his first feature film lead role. Anxiously, he unpacked. With lines learnt, he wondered whether he would be able to carry the weight of the film on his shoulders. The cast and crew were fantastic and the blocking of the first scene was underway after an initial table read the night before. Jack readied himself as the final checks were called in before the first take.

Hair and make up artists fussed around his face as the costume department straightened the bottom of his shirt. With the actors checked, ready on their marks, the assistant director announced they were rolling as the director called the first "ACTION" from his chair at the monitor. The morning was a huge success, they had made a terrific start. The doubts cleared in his mind. This was his time to shine.

# # #

A missed call appeared on Evelyn's mobile as she drove to work for a meeting which parted the news that the contract at the studios where she worked wasn't going to be renewed. She sat hopelessly on the bed in her apartment. There was only one person she wanted to talk to in this desolate state, overrun by her emotions she dialed his number.

Recently back from four weeks filming, he answered hearing her upset.

"What's wrong? Evelyn what's happened?" Jack tendered to her softly. He knew her better than anyone, even when they weren't in conscious conversation, they sensed each other's feelings.

"I'm coming home," she replied.

She explained the contract for her filming was due to finish. She would have to leave her apartment and head back to London. Gently he talked to her, calming her, reassuring her.

"Come and stay with me this weekend. You know this is a blessing in disguise, Evelyn. It is all meant to be. We can be together properly now. Come and live with me. Let's give it a go."

"Really?" Evelyn wasn't convinced questioning him with vulnerability. "You want that?"

"Yes."

The world was set right once more. The unknown destination from this life changing blow had now been positively redecorated. They had decided to commit to each other.

# # #

Chapter 27

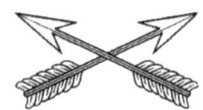

The sun shone brightly through the kitchen window as Jack happily made them lunch, anticipating Evelyn's arrival for the weekend. They were both excited to discuss their new plans. Jack romantically laid the garden table, pouring the wine as he placed the plates on the top of the wooden picnic bench. The legs of the table had been planted firmly in the brown mud in the big garden. A clean and healthy lunch of avocado, mozzarella and tomato plus a helping of pesto was complemented with a refreshing glass of rose wine.

Evelyn drove with a smile as she got closer to Jack's house. A sense of danger mixed with an addictive happiness moving through her as the radio played. While parking she noticed he wasn't waiting for her and there was no sign of him in the house. Pushing open the front door she caught sight of Jack at the table in the freshly mowed garden, her lunch and her man ready and waiting in the sunshine. She glowed with happiness.

After their lunch, Evelyn asked Jack to retrieve a package from her car. A large gift, wrapped in birthday present paper. She hadn't forgotten. Jack was excited, lifting it out carefully as he carried it inside grinning like a little boy. He liked to play the guessing game. His hands pressed around the edges, squashing it gently. Evelyn impatient for him to open it. A smart sleek North Face suitcase revealed itself as Jack ripped the present from the paper.

"It's for when you have to fly off around the world filming," she said. "So I will always be able to travel with you."

"I love it, Evelyn." He kissed her on the forehead, holding her tightly in his arms.

In the afternoon, a nap was required and they cuddled up like a perfect puzzle piece along the length of the sofa. The warm sun beating through the window as they dozed off to sleep, Evelyn nestled in Jack's arms. The nap led to wandering hands and Jack carried her upstairs as they showered each other's bodies with kind kisses.

Waking up they both began to re- energize. Leading the two of them back downstairs, Jack headed towards the stereo with a wild need for music. He danced like a mad man with the dog jumping up at him from all the excitement. Evelyn sat at the kitchen table in his t-shirt, her bare legs crossed over one another, smiling on at him with a huge open heart. The song played loudly from the cd player as he sung out the lyrics from the bottom of his lungs.

"I'm coming out..." a masculine version of the Diana Ross classic, complimented with camp dance moves in an unforgettable private performance.

The next day, after another long night of excited bedroom activity, Jack had bits and bobs to attend to and

Evelyn came along for the ride. He was fixing up a house he had rented out and trips to the faithful hardware stores were a necessity. After the jobs were completed Jack started his journey home, or so Evelyn thought.

The sun shone brightly over a bowling green that was fenced off decoratively. The professional green lay in and among a square of beautifully kept houses, very much resembling something from an expensive area in central London. The building accompanying the green was white fronted, the entrance accompanied by shiny black Victorian railings. The bowls green was immaculately kept. Nearest to the green and at the back of the pure white building was a quaint cafe which had a pink and white striped awning used to add to the authentic feel and to protect the outside tables from any unexpected showers. It seemed like the sort of place that would miss the rain. Even if the raging winds that brushed off from the sea attempted to shower the seaside town with a downpour, somehow this spot would, like a crop circle, be protected from the elements.

Jack parked the car, opening the cute tearoom cafe door for Evelyn. "I thought you might like it in here."

She did. It was quintessentially English. The handcrafted English bone China teapots, cups and saucers, waited pompously, ready to be presented from behind the wooden topped counter. The scones were presented with pristine precision, freshly made and dusted with icing sugar. Their faithful jam pots sitting at the perfect distance by their mouthwatering side. On the back wall, behind the cotton white, tabard wearing tearoom host, was a traditional black chalk board articulately detailing today's menu.

Instructed to take their seats, they found a little table and settled in to their surroundings as the tearoom waitress came to take their order. A plastic white numbered square was left in the small silver stand on the table top. Jack looked on, admiring her beauty as Evelyn smiled in the simple but romantic setting.

Leaving them with their cups of tea, the waitress saw Jack look into Evelyn's brown eyes. He couldn't quite work her out but he concluded that his burning desire to do so must be positive.

"I really love you, Evelyn Wise," his words kind and soft. A moment passed as they took it in.

"You know I would never hurt you don't you, Jack? I couldn't even if I wanted to."

They breathed into the honesty, settling into the pause of this moment. With cheshire cat smiles they gleamed at each other and then looked away, embarrassed at their vulnerabilities as the waitress placed two thick slices of freshly homemade Victoria Sponge cake on the intimately sized table. Their silverware sparkled as they sipped their tea, the supplementary Victoria sponge crumbling softly in their mouths.

Evelyn wouldn't say anything today. This moment was too special and she wasn't one hundred percent sure that Jack's reaction would be positive.

She was late.

# # #

Chapter 28

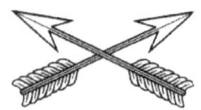

She was sure it was just the stress of everything. It wasn't their main priority today. She would keep a close eye on her body clock over the next few days and if the situation didn't change, she would chat to Jack about her concerns.

Two older woman wearing white bowls attire flipped a two pence piece. Walking towards the playing field, one rolled the jack to the other end of the green to serve as a target. Smiling, in love, Jack and Evelyn walked passed the iron fencing laughing happily, hands held as they returned to the car.

Evelyn sat on a broken swing in the freshly mowed green garden, her laptop rested on her thighs. Giggling to herself at a YouTube video she was watching, content, peaceful. She decided she would tell Jack this evening about being late. It was, after all his doing as well as hers.

With Evelyn making herself at home after his proposal to move in, now that her contract was coming to a close and she would be moving closer to him again, Jack's mind begun to cloud his thoughts with doubts as she positively discussed how their new arrangement could work well.

He really wasn't sure this was the right move. The words were streaming from her mouth. If Evelyn were to move in, his routines would be altered and his haven would now be intruded. He loved having her there but what if it didn't work? A triad of doubts built one on top of the other as his internal state became rapidly tense and closed off. Unaware of this, Evelyn called playfully to him to join her in watching the YouTube video. Jack watched in silence before his doubting state began surfacing quickly and uncontrollably from within him.

His lips uttered the fateful blow. "I don't think this is going to work, Evelyn." Jack uttered it quietly, carefully.

"What do mean its not going to work...?" Evelyn replied cautiously.

"This...us...we're two different people, worlds apart." The sun hid behind the only cloud that sat in the sky that day as Evelyn tried to remain calm, adrenaline pumping through her veins.

"You're too young, immature...you need to find someone your own age." He was surprised by his own words as they continued, penetrating her soul. As the sentences left his lips he knew the pain he had caused, her eyes reflecting her hurting heart. "I think you should leave," he went on.

Evelyn sat like a statue, her mind still trying to frantically process the new information. "Who do you think you are, Jack?" Evelyn raised her voice, he stood shocked. "Everything is always on your terms. I have to come to you. I phone you. I am here to stroke your ego when you need a boost of self confidence," she continued.

Jack walked strongly up the bare stairs and retrieved her things from the bedroom, moving quickly onto the next room, collecting her toiletries from the bathroom and throwing them into her bag. "It is time you went home. Get your stuff and leave."

There was no reasoning with him when he was like this. Nothing she could have said or done that would change his mind in this irrational and made up mind state.

Evelyn took a deep breath fighting the ocean of emotion that built inside her, tears restrained in the wells of her eyes.

"Why are you fighting this when I am telling you to leave Evelyn?" He shouted.

"Because I love you and I thought you loved me," she replied through held back tears.

"You don't understand what love is," he stated.

"Why are you saying this, where has this come from? Jack, you would make the best father and husband. I do love you. Please stop this; this is crazy."

"I might, but right now I don't want to be with anyone. I am happier on my own. Please, just leave." Jack passed her on the landing, walking downstairs with her bags he had packed.

There was nothing else to say but he ended it with a fateful blow, "I love you, but I'm not in love with you."

The world stopped. Closing the door behind her as soon as she left, a screaming rage boiled inside him. Jack sat silently on his soft sofa. A single tear falling from each of his tired and watering pupils. The arguing was echoing loudly in his stifling mind. What had he done? He knew how stubborn she was. She wouldn't be back after this. He had lost her forever.

Jack's dog looked up at the hollow shell of a man. Jack yearned to be loved and questioned why he couldn't let Evelyn in. He knew she could give him what he wanted and her heart was huge. No one could love him or make love to him like Evelyn did. She had hit some raw notes in the midst of the argument, so had he. They had expertly listened to every detail the other had said over the time they had spent together. The good and the bad. The ammunition was stored and ready for this occasion. The prevailing of these pertinent personal attacks now stained the lips that once whispered loving words from purer hearts.

# # #

She shouldn't have been driving. A blur of orange and yellow traffic cones paved the route in front of her. The light of her headlight bulbs fading fast and eventually going out completely. Driving without headlights on the busiest motorway in England wasn't a priority. Her heart was in two. Her hands gripped the steering wheel intently focusing on the guiding cats eyes in the road identifying the separate lanes on the motorway. Why wouldn't he ever talk? They never communicated properly when things got tough. They became closed off. They shut down.

She was infuriated. Tears streamed from her face exiting towards home. Evelyn's car pulled up to her parent's house. Her sister opened the front door as Evelyn fell into her loving arms. Evelyn was now a hollow shell of a woman.

# # #

Jack descended into a week long depression. Evelyn's words repeating in his mind. Action was needed. A dramatic change, but what? Sleeping was the only answer. His dog was by his side amongst the mountain of other problems that cluttered his life.

# # #

The drive back to her apartment was longer than usual. Every memory bleeding into her stifled brain as she returned. A short block of filming remained and then she was finished. It was difficult saying goodbye to the people she had work with every day for two years. She had built a new family up at the studios. Jack had messaged to say he would help, if she needed any, moving her things back down. His intentionally kind gesture only added salt to the wound.

He intuitively knew she would decline the offer. Evelyn tried to embrace the occasion to sort through the items she had acquired, reflecting happily on her time in her apartment, giggling to herself as she remembered certain instances that had happened there.

With all the emotional turmoil, Evelyn's mind had been elsewhere. Promptly it returned to focusing on her body clock. No change. That afternoon Evelyn decided that she needed to purchase a pregnancy test and wandered into town to collect one in between the packing up of her things. She told herself not to worry as she queued up in the line at the pharmacy, her heart beating loudly from her panicking chest.

The walk back to her apartment was slow as she attempted to silence the fears her mother had installed in her. The lift in her block was out of order today, maintenance work made the stairs the only access to reaching her apartment on the top floor.

Evelyn entered the key in the lock of the front door turning it with ease, placing her handbag just inside the door. The penthouse apartment hallway was now a maze of boxes in anticipation of her official moving date as she made her way into the bathroom to do the test. Reading the instructions carefully she was informed that her fate would be decided in the next two minutes. One hundred and twenty seconds later it was. She was pregnant with Jack's child.

Evelyn wept confused on her bathroom floor. Jack had told her how he felt and he had meant it. She couldn't have a child with a man who wasn't in love with her. Now that her acting job had finished she also had no way to provide for this child. Not in the way she would have wanted to. She had dreamt of giving them a wealth of luxuries, a life where money wouldn't be the permanent struggle.

Evelyn loved children; her heart broke as her inner voice whispered the wisest decision. She would research her options for a termination in the morning. Evelyn cried the rest of that day, her world stalling. With her heart feeling a pain she never thought she could endure, that night she cried herself to sleep, praying for Jack to call.

The silence between them continued as a lonely Christmas loomed. Evelyn completed her packing and was due to move back in with her parents, the original plan to live with Jack making the loss of her own space even more unbearable. Evelyn's life was boxed and packed up once more as she singlehandedly carried her luggage to the car. She vowed never to return to his house. Jack King had to disappear from her every thought.

Unaware of Evelyn's strife, Jack took massive action, clearing his house from top to bottom, ready to rent it out and start over, financially and emotionally. He called his brother and asked politely to use the space in a barn that he had on his farmland. His brother used it to store other bits and pieces and Jack was sure he wouldn't mind him having some of his things there, just until he got himself sorted.

Evelyn and Jack were both determined to learn from this heartache. They began to take the first steps alone, with open hearts their confident exteriors masked their vulnerability. Their souls quietly calling the others name in the shards of silence that sliced in amongst the chaos.

# # #

Chapter 29

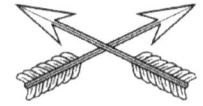

The New Year's celebrations offered a wealth of hope as fresh plans were implemented and looked forward too. Evelyn had visited her family doctor on her return and two pills had removed Jack and Evelyn's child. Evelyn cried as she swallowed the tablets. Her dreams of their children jumping for joy on them in their big bed in their renovated warehouse apartment were removed permanently.

Evelyn needed to get away. A new perspective on life beckoned. She took a trip to the mountains, resting in the solitude of the fresh air. Returning to her room after a day on the slopes, a message flashed up on her phone. Jack King. It had been many months without a word. Evelyn decided it was better to continue the silence between them. At least until she returned.

They planned a friendly catch up. The smell of an enormous amount of brand new books greeted Jack as he entered the beauty of the book shop. Best selling novels were presented to him as he walked through the silence of the library like shop which set the scene for the pair to reunite amongst the unread love stories.

He took the elevator to the top of world class Waterstones book shop in Piccadilly Circus. A three hundred and sixty degree view of London circulated the central bar through the glass windows as he settled himself in the laid back, black leather chair to wait for Evelyn to arrive. His experience of hiding his anxiety towards the up and coming meeting had been professionally trained through his audition practice. Jack ordered a coffee from the passing barman.

Evelyn's stomach was slightly knotted with butterflies in excitement and a nervous anticipation at the unknown expectation of this particular meeting. She, however, was still relaxed from her retreat from the mountains. Casually she pressed the button in the lift to instruct it to take her to the top floor. The silver doors opened as Jack's head turned and Evelyn caught his smiling eyes. He rose from his chair to warmly greet her. She was distant today and a strong guard was ever present as he asked her to move her chair closer to him, which she refused confirming the distance was fine for her.

Evelyn questioned her thoughts about the older man in front of her and for the first time she began to feel nothing. She had developed an expertly trained personal numbness towards everything that echoed his name. She found it much easier this way. In that instance Evelyn decided it was right to continue with her life without Jack.

She wanted something more, her heart deserved more than scraps of his love and time. This moment confirmed to her that other options were more appealing. He did not meet her needs.

Jack, on the other hand, sat focused on the girl in front of him, enjoying her company. The meeting was pleasantly ended after a crisp glass of white wine as they headed off without a kiss. Their separate pathways led out of the huge glassed double doors of the paramount entrance of the Waterstones shop on Regents Street.

The contact was very sparse between them after this meeting. A quiet year and three months pasted as the snow melted on the cobblestones of Shaftesbury Avenue, the ice water trickling into the iron grated drains down from the curbs of the pavements. Daffodil bulbs expanded under the grounds of the lavish green communal parks, their shoots now confident enough to make their way up to the slightly warmer surface.

For a week he played on her mind solidly, as she batted the thoughts away with the one thousand reasons why he was not in her life. A text message left her phone. He replied.

It was May again. Four years since Jack and Evelyn's paths had originally met behind the stage door. A recently washed shiny red mx5 sports car pulled up outside a broad brick house. In the far left hand corner a home she once spent many happy memories in still housed a handful of cars awaiting attention.

It was very strange being back in Jack's neck of the woods. A matching pair of painted red nails turned the key in the ignition, resting the car's engine after its drive.

A tall dark haired man nervously mowed the lawn awaiting the arrival of someone he once loved. Evelyn locked the car and walked confidently to the door, her stomach seemed to have dropped out from underneath her body, her palms beginning to sweat in sync. Jack Wise's mother, an older woman in her late sixties opened the door to Evelyn, welcoming her in, as two dogs excitedly jumped up around her legs, scratching Evelyn who attempted to hold her cool composure.

He sensed she was here. He had done everything he could to try and forget her. He turned off the lawnmower talking himself together and walked cooly back inside, smiling at the attractive young woman he now barely recognised. For a few moments the two of them stood in silence, the entire world slowing down around them. He could hear his heart beat reverberating around his ear drums. Her breathing felt like a gale force wind as every breath was taken away by this addictive moment.

Noticing the silence needed to be filled for her own comfortability, the older woman offered a cup of tea to Evelyn who politely replied that a glass of water would do. Her mouth was now excruciatingly dry.

"Let's go for a walk." The only words that could spring to Jack's mind in this overpowering reunion. Evelyn chatted thankfully to the older women as Jack ran upstairs to fetch his trainers.

They walked like they had done so many times before, side by side, the sounds of the sea settling them both into each other's company. This walk was very different as hands were strategically kept to themselves, both of them holding their own individual ground. He appeared calm, she together. Neither of them internally experiencing these outward attributes.

Jack discovered Evelyn was learning to ride a motorbike to top up her acting skill set. It was something that Jack was proficient in. She didn't have her license, but expressed her desire to practice.

"Hey if you have time today I have a bike. Do you fancy a little ride?" Jack enquired hopefully. They always united in adventure and spontaneity, two qualities they loved in each other.

"Yes, of course. That would be great, thanks!"

Hopping in their individual soft top cars, roofs down as the summer sun blazed onto the crazy twosome, they raced through the country lanes like a blockbuster movie car chase. The tall banks of green hedges guided them down the skinny roads until they reached a wooden gated farm housing a small bungalow and large, white wooden barn.

The gravel crunched under their tyres as they drove up. Parking her car, Evelyn curiously examined her surroundings, even after all this time, she still didn't trust Jack; she didn't really trust anyone.

"The bike's in here," Jack said enthusiastically pointing to the barn.

Wheeling a strong red motorcross bike out of its shelter, he kick started the engine, handing a helmet to Evelyn as he pushed it towards the land that they would use as their practice place. Evelyn got on the bike as Jack then climbed on and nestled up behind her. Their bodies touching for the first time in a long time as the engine roared from underneath them. Sitting behind her Jack reached round and placed his strong masculine hands over hers, instructing her on how to accelerate and brake on this particular model of bike. His heart was pressed up to her back in the very close proximity. The engine vocalized as Evelyn got used to the gears, Jack instructing her over the noise, his lips dangerously close to her neck.

With her confidence built up, he was able to take his hands away from hers and rested them at home on her hips. They laughed as the speed increased and they lapped around the fenced field, then progressing into confident figure eights.

After the motorbike ride, Jack was excited to show her the white wooden barn which was piled high with his stuff. After all this time Evelyn had convinced herself that she didn't love him anymore. It was always black and white with her, she couldn't deal with things any other way. She felt this until the next thing he said.

They stood side by side in the barn. Alone without the world watching. The silence of the countryside in harmony with the stillness of the barn as their hearts opened in the uncensored comfort of the other. It had taken all day and up until this silence to connect fully to the other. "I want to clear this out, make a warehouse apartment, complete with the top bit as a bedroom and balcony level looking down," Jack announced softly. This is what they talked of over dinner in Soho that night, reaching a conclusion of the visual image of their ideal home together. In those conversations, in addition to detailing and looking at the materialistic things they would have and the vision of the house itself, Jack had intricately described his vision of their daily life.

Evelyn would be having her singing lessons downstairs around the grand piano whilst he would be upstairs looking down over the balcony with a beaming smile and a cup of freshly brewed coffee. She dreamed of cooking family meals in the open plan kitchen, their children quietly watching their parents in blockbuster award winning movies on the wide plasma screen as they lay casually outstretched on giant beanbags fueled with inspiration.

Evelyn wanted to see Jack working out in the gym from the balcony above as the organic smells from the kitchen announced the arrival of dinner. It was the complete image of the life they wanted, the dream. They would walk into town from their location in Covent Garden for castings returning successfully to their little hub of happiness.

For the next few minutes as Jack described the plans he had for the barn, they were gone, drifting once more into their ideal life. The universe listening. He looked over at her, wanting to pick her up and tell her they would have this one day, kiss her to the floor and make love in their visualized new home right there and then, as if it were real, as if they could have it. Their eyes locked, Evelyn smiling up him.

A ringing sound broke the silence of the dreamers. Evelyn's agent rang, the only call that she wouldn't avoid in this blissful moment.

"It's my agent..."

He wanted to hold onto that moment as if his life depended on it and tell her he would find the money to make it happen, but he also knew the importance of this call for her.

"Take it, take it." Jack insisted smiling excitedly for her.

She was such a free spirit and he loved this about her. She wasn't scared. She needed to grow and had the world at her feet. He told himself it wasn't fair for him to stop her. She would live a fulfilling life. Jack always thought Evelyn had everything. She did, except the one thing she really wanted, Jack.

She sat on the farm fence, the sun shining down on her. Evelyn was positively radiating with excitement. Jack watched lovingly as he leaned against his new car. She listened as her agent delivered her news of two auditions she had set up for Evelyn, including a huge feature film role. Climbing down off the wooden fence, Evelyn knew her friend was waiting for her arrival at her house near by. It was time to say goodbye again.

It almost seemed as if they had only just began to adjust to one another's company as Jack said goodbye, expressing it over the roof of his car. He looked over at her, his heart beating vulnerably as he watched her smile at him and get into her car about to drive away. A sight he had seen all too often.

Evelyn followed Jack off the farm and down the country lanes in their separate cars, turning off as they reached the motorway and she was gone again. Typically in the days that followed their meetings a number of proceeding text messages and a phone call or two would occur and then the silence reentered between them.

The intense emotions were always too much to articulate. The time had coated their pure love in cobwebs of events and other people. It was always easier to protect their hearts and say nothing. The fear of rejection was more powerful than allowing the success of their love to prevail. If only they could each make that extra step. Once more, the silent retreat was seemingly more comfortable for both of them.

# # #

Chapter 30

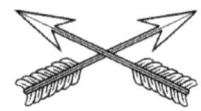

Halloween was approaching and so was Evelyn's pre pilot season trip to Los Angeles. It would be a busy time in the American television and film industry from January to April as the town geared up for the mass casting of the new television scripts that had made the cut this year. Actors all hoped to be picked as the excitement brewed and the profile names were attached to the projects. October would be an ideal time to test the ropes and see if coming back in January was what she ultimately wanted to do.

As Evelyn left Heathrow for her American adventure she decided to reopen her heart fully to a new man that would love her unconditionally. Heathrow airport welcomed Evelyn and her luggage. Its international terminal was a holding space of opportunity for thousands. A crisp clean white boarding pass to LAX was printed from a kind ground staff member of the efficient airline. Evelyn held it firmly in her hand, the golden ticket to her next chapter.

#

The sharply, steam ironed, cabin crew, were dressed impeccably. The female flight attendants' dress code requiring their hair to be kept firmly on their heads. Evelyn observed their buns that were dotted down the plane aisles which were sprayed perfectly in their pruned place. The crew bustled in the aisles as Evelyn planned her afternoon of movie watching from the skies. Stretching her legs, she walked down the long and skinny aisle, a pathway between passengers, to the toilets. In front of her stood a tall man over six foot with noticeably attractive arms, a weakness to Evelyn at the best of times.

They shared a couple of fleeting gazes as they both waited patiently in the unusually long line. Evelyn nervously focused herself. The man, ever more aware of the energy she was omitting towards him, smiled. His blue eyes warming to her. Both of them were dressed smart but comfortably in their relaxed plane wear and the man could not help glancing at Evelyn's toned legs in her leggings.

"Hi" the man blushed. Evelyn knew he was older than she, probably older than Jack or of a similar age. She knew immediately he was an actor. Jack had had his hair cut short but this man had the type of hair she loved. Dark and short but a bit on the longer side, the length where men usually get it cut but is just right to run your fingers through when sharing a passionate kiss.

"Hi," Evelyn sweetly replied. For some reason she had expected him to be American but he was english too and spoke very well, Evelyn later discovering he had studied Law at university. They hit it off immediately sharing their experiences of L.A., the man a world of acting knowledge, Evelyn an inspiration to him.

They exchanged contacts and arranged to meet up to continue their conversation in the city of angels.

Excitedly they returned to their individual seats as the movie research alternated between reading and napping. Touching down in Los Angeles the passengers departed the plane and headed for baggage claim and immigration.

James Hunt, the man from the plane, scanned the hundreds of other passengers for Evelyn. Two rows behind him, Evelyn wheeled her black case. The people in the lines advanced slowly to receive their stamps from immigration. Evelyn and James cheekily caught each other's eyes through the gaps in between the people. A moment that Evelyn would later cherish.

Blessed Evelyn took a traditional yellow cab from LAX to Santa Monica, staying in her favorite hotel on the seafront. Jet lagged, she ran a bath and relaxed onto the king sized bed of her hotel suite. Undressing, her body succumbed to the heat of the water as she reflected on how happy she was in this moment.

The meetings began immediately the next day as Evelyn went from one casting director introduction to the next. As the days crept on Evelyn worked hard embracing and navigating the alienation of the culture against her own. One night Evelyn embraced the occasion to suspend herself from the demands of work and meet with a friend for a night out of food, partying and fun. It was this night she met the man who would show her the meaning of real love for the first time.

# # #

Chapter 31

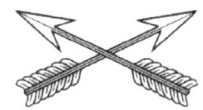

The vintage looking bar was overly crowded on the popular Abbot Kinney stretch in Venice Beach as Evelyn and her friends entered the hip and laid back watering hole. Evelyn rested by a table as two men chatted beside her. He caught her eye playfully and reverted to his conversation. A few fun hours passed as Evelyn continued to chat with her friends and sip wine. They laughed about the events of her trip thus far until her conversation over spilled into his.

He was a doctor, but not in the conventional sense. He was fun with an exciting zest for life which Evelyn fell for immediately and for the first time, she fully forgot about Jack.

The three busy weeks of work began filling up with dates in between as a brand new love began to ripen. He treated her like royalty, wining and dining her across Los Angeles. Being the ultimate gentleman Evelyn became to worry if he had lost interest as unlike the forward focused men she had known she was climbing the walls for a kiss. The one thing she really loved was that she trusted him, she didn't know if it was because he was a doctor but he always knew the right thing to say.

They both had had busy days as he waited outside his cool bachelor beach house as she pulled up. Returning to the trunk of the car to gather her things, he helped carry them in, his free hand holding hers. She was inwardly impressed by his apartment and thoroughly enjoyed being romanced by him. A healthy dinner was ready, accompanied by a rich red wine. Evelyn was due to fly home the next day. After dinner the couple cuddled up once he had casually handed her a pair of her very own blue scrubs, something to remember him by. They lay in their snug scrubs on the sofa as the Californian sun settled leaving a warm twilight trailing in through the open windows. She loaded up her car for the airport smiling at his Harvard certificates mounted on the wall.

# # #

Chapter 32

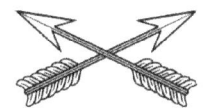

Winter had settled over London. The lights of the Millennium bridge lit up the River Thames as cute Christmas markets roasted festive chestnuts. An old man stood over the coals wearing dirty black, fingerless gloves.

He looked towards the traditionally coloured carousel at the shiny horses moving up and down to the classical sounds of the fairground music. He looked at a young woman on the merry go round laughing with a smaller little girl, perhaps her own daughter. She looked just like Evelyn.

His mind wandered fondly, a dull ache in his unfulfilled heart. She was getting older now and he considered the thought of her having children with another man, bringing a sick feeling to his gut and a lump in his throat. He looked on and felt for his phone, scrolling through his phone book for her number.

The crowded market swarmed around him, people pushing past him as he placed his phone back in his pocket, continuing on. He looked towards a hog roast stand and fondly thought about when he and Evelyn had crackling pork baps overflowing with apple sauce--a Christmas when the hope of spending it together felt alive and new.

Unbeknownst to Jack, Evelyn was crossing the Waterloo bridge up above while sending a delayed text message reply to him. In it she detailed she was moving to America and that she was seeing someone else. While his reply was positive, underneath the words his heart sunk; she was leaving for good.

He wanted to ask her to stay but he knew to do so was selfish and he didn't want to stop her from doing what she needed to do.

Evelyn received the reply and smiled. Deep down all she ever wanted was him to fight for her, to tell her to stay. She would have done so. Now, she had to get on with her life, a new life on the other side of the world, away from Jack.

The winter wind blew in his face as he stood looking out across the Thames while contemplating Evelyn's departure.

Evelyn packed up her belongings. Her life now residing in one large suitcase and some hand luggage. Jack knew the date of the flight which stuck out prominently in his mind leading up to her departure. Evelyn preferred not to say goodbyes and after procrastinating on it, by the time it was time to leave, she had barely told a soul she was going. One of her best friends called her as she was on the way to the airport to ask if it were true.

She laughed casually stating in the words of Arnold Schwarnezgner, "I'll be back." But the truth was, this time she had booked a one-way flight, a brave and more permanent move.

He looked at the clock on the mantelpiece while slouched on the sofa in his gym clothes. Today was the day. She would leave for good. He thought last time she moved away from London that she seemed far from him. This time it wouldn't be a few hours in the car at the opposite end of the country. She would be living on the other side of the world.

As he stirred his porridge he contemplated calling her mobile and decided against it. She would be busy saying goodbye to her family or wheeling her luggage. She wouldn't have time to talk to him and then he would feel foolish for phoning. He regretted not calling the evening before or the week before. He sat silently listening to his intuition.

Evelyn enjoyed a hearty English breakfast in the airport cafe reflecting on the bold journey and new chapter ahead while savoring a final taste of home comforts. A long text message arrived on her phone from Jack. In it he wished her a safe journey and happiness in her new life. Evelyn boarded the plane without looking back.

# # #

Chapter 33

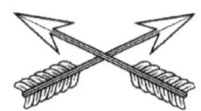

Having charmed the cabin crew, Evelyn had enjoyed the flight from business class. A enjoyable journey of rest in a spacious environment filled with delicate sandwiches and unlimited chocolate truffles. She felt the world at her feet as she stepped off the plane in Los Angeles. She was back in business. A huge smile emerged from her youthful face as the sun beamed down.

Her internet movie data base picture, stained Jack's computer screen. He could barely remember the warm touch of her naked chest pressed up against his. He yearned to innocently kiss her forehead and rest his head in her lap on the sofa in front of a film she picked, which he only watched because she wanted to. Things were improving for him in his career. The credits were building; he was getting where he needed to be, but there was something missing. The hole in the puzzle. Evelyn Wise. He knew the world would know her name, but he knew it before the world. She was, and will always be the little beauty that walked into his dressing room that day.

Evelyn loved being in L.A. It breathed a new lease of life into her. The cool Pacific Ocean air harmonized with the blazing, all year round, summer sunshine. She was in her element surrounded by her own kind. Runners lined the morning sidewalks of Ocean Avenue as Evelyn jogged down the famous Santa Monica steps and out towards the ocean. The golden sand collided with her bare feet as she took off her running sneakers and continued her jog along the water's edge. The white foam from the ridge of the waves crashed at her feet, enjoying being bathed by its coolness. The perfect start to the morning.

She grabbed a vitamin infused, all natural juice from a juice bar as she neared her apartment for a cool down stroll before hitting the shower. Meetings and auditions were timetabled into very busy weeks as Evelyn successfully met with casting directors and directors all over town.

The age of technology was booming, consequently impressing itself upon the process of auditioning for actors. In their rooms on opposite sides of the world Jack and Evelyn fiddled with the camera's on their mac laptop computers angling the screens as they stood in view of the inbuilt cameras. Scripts lay scribbled on side tables, hoping they would not be called upon for lines that had not fully embedded themselves in their subconscious. The record button illuminated from the screen and the links were emailed to their agents.

The most difficult part of auditioning for both of them was letting it go after it was done as not to disrupt the process with detrimental thoughts from the ego. Evelyn opted for a frozen yoghurt, Jack an expresso.

Jack emailed Evelyn, wanting her to receive his well wishes on her immediate arrival. He missed her already. It had started to sink in that he would never see her again.

Thoughts of Jack provided a home comfort as Evelyn battled daily with change. Nothing seemed familiar. The language, even though the same, was worlds apart and the culture although blissful, was an adjustment that would take time to adapt to.

Jack spoke to Evelyn on a Sunday after yoga, her voice soft and calming. He asked her if she needed anything English to remind her of home and offered to send her out some Cadbury's chocolates to keep her spirits up at her request. She didn't think he would. A couple of weeks later they arrived. With the distance, the chocolates felt like an evening with his arm around her as she watched a movie, enjoying the treats on a rare evening in the apartment.

Jack's phone rang with some exciting news from his agent. He had booked it! A fantastic new acting role which would be flying him out next week to film. He tapped the red button to end the call and put down his phone to execute an ecstatic celebratory dance. This would be huge.

Evelyn loved Santa Monica Sundays, a rested morning after which she strolled to join her fellow yogis at practice. A chance to reflect on the previous week, goal planning in her focused mind for the week ahead.

Jack had left a voicemail for Evelyn that week, her response still unknown. It was rare for him to phone her, but she loved it when he did. One of the reasons why she had confirmed to herself that leaving Jack behind was a good idea was that he lacked one quality she knew she needed, reliability. A peaceful smile softened her face as she dialed his landline number against the chattering voices in her mind that told her not to. His voice cut in as the ringing ended.

"Hello?"

"Hello, Jack."

A bittersweet silence entered the line as Jack adjusted his composure knowing instantly the voice at the other end.

"Hello, little one. How are you?"

She spoke softly, rested and heartfelt. They laughed as they always did, the conversation effortless. They had missed one another a great deal, the eagerness in their voices highlighting much more than what was said.

It was a very busy time for the industry in Los Angeles and at home. The television networks fought for finances deciding on which pilot would get picked up. Evelyn's auditioning experience at this time was a long way out of her comfort zone. The phone rang and she was given the news that she had been recalled for a project she had self taped and sent to her agent a few weeks back.

The audition waiting room was filled with beautiful faces. The sign in sheet full with names listed one on top of the other as Evelyn approached the desk. They were running a long way behind on the schedule. She must remain firmly focused on the target of booking this job. No matter how long it took. Others would wilt with tiredness. She had come too far to surrender to laziness now.

Weeks passed without a word. The silence usually defining a resounding no from the opportunity presented. Evelyn parked her car, meeting a friend for lunch. He was a kind soul and enjoyed her company. Her friend nudged her as he noticed an Oscar award winning actress seated in the same restaurant with her daughter. Distracted by the phone, Evelyn took the call. She had been waiting on the outcome of a feature film audition. Her agent delivered the news that she hadn't received the role but that she had been offered a role in a new television show, the one she had self taped two months ago. Her feet lifted from the ground as she jumped for joy, the rest of the restaurant sharing in the excitement.

Evelyn was to film her new show ironically in Europe and returned to England for a week in between filming for the new U.S. show she had just booked.

Evelyn loved being back in London. While on the way to a casting director meeting, she walked past the coffee shop near Jack's agent's office and fleetingly gazed inside on the off chance that he might be there. She had emailed him the previous night, but was unable to receive his reply on her temporary English number with no internet connection.

Jack King knew she was in town. He wandered happily into his regular coffee shop emailing Evelyn back, optimistic by the prospect that he may see her. Seated with a friend, he willed for a reply on his phone. Hours passed without a word.

Evelyn arrived home, sitting down with a cup of tea as she logged into her emails. A message from Jack sat at the top of her inbox. The email invited her to meet him for coffee in the shop she had gazed briefly into just two hours before. They had missed one another by a few minutes. The UK stop over came and went as Evelyn boarded a plane back to America.

# # #

Chapter 34

A car picked Jack up from his home in the early hours of a March morning. He wheeled the suitcase that Evelyn had bought him toward it. All the struggle and his hard work now felt worth it as the past was put behind him and he relaxed back into the leather seats.

The sun began to rise as Jack looked through the front windscreen, the wide open motorway carless up ahead. A blue signpost directed the driver to Heathrow airport as Jack felt like a kid on Christmas Eve.

# # #

Even though Evelyn had been filming, her finances were looking positively negative and she needed a job to fund herself in between her auditioning and securing her next acting job. The glamour of acting is often short lived when the harsh face of reality rears its ugly head and survival becomes the main priority.

Evelyn breathed in deeply, bracing herself for the undesired task that loomed. Two large American women waddled towards her as she got out of her car and walked the green mile towards the dreary apartment complex. The paintwork was outdated, well, everything was and it was in desperate need of being rescued from the eighties.

The overweight woman smiled as Evelyn felt like Matilda meeting Miss Trunchbull.

"So you can clean these condos while I'm away in Vegas, yes?"

"Yes, of course" Evelyn replied crying behind the plastered on smile, her soul crumbling.

The overweight owner walked Evelyn around the rooms, instructing her on how to make a bed, sweep a floor and fold a towel. Evelyn nodded as she listened to the painfully laborious instructions that seemed to never end. She knew it was only temporary, a matter of a couple of weeks, a means to an end, part of the process, but she couldn't help wanting to be anywhere other than here. In fact she didn't tell anyone she was doing it. Ashamed that if she even admitted it to one person, saying it out loud would make it real. If she didn't tell anyone, it wouldn't be real. She would get the cash and go.

As Evelyn looked under the dirty bed, the mounds of hair and dust made her gag. She knew if she was a man even Jack's drug dealing world might be a more appealing part-time career choice.

To stay sane Evelyn plugged in her headphones, listening to the lessons in acting and voice work, anything to take away from the reality of the work she had taken on.

A guest in his late seventies sat outside his apartment escaping the nagging of his wife who called him from inside the condo with her agonizingly dull American drawl. His wrinkled bare red chest fried in the sun like a huge grisly fat pork chop, sweat dripping from his grey-haired, sagging pecs.

"You don't look like a cleaner."

Noticing his lips move, although unable to hear him over the sound of the YouTube audio acting tutorials that played on her iphone, Evelyn politely replied, "Sorry?"

"I said you don't look like a cleaner."

The words landed on Evelyn who mustered up the courage to say through a dream shattering heart and a lump in her throat.

"I'm not." A half smile concealed her screaming inside. "I'm an actress."

The man's reaction was all too common.

"Of course you are," he jested. "Don't they all say that in Hollywood?" With a burning heart and tears held back Evelyn smiled.

"Apparently so," she joked back. Continuing to carry the dirty bed linen to the washer/dryer.

# # #

Chapter 35

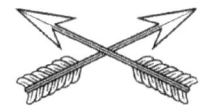

Evelyn felt upbeat as she drove out for a rare night of socialising. Singing to herself as she cruised in the car, she arrived at her destination and buzzed her arrival at their gate before entering the secluded drive and then making her way up the cobblestone steps to the front door.

She knew she should, but Evelyn rarely watched television. It was, however, something her friends enjoyed tremendously. As the wine was poured the television was flicked on...an escape from life. Evelyn nestled comfortably on the sofa, her friends happy to see her rest.

As the final dinner preparations were being readied, Evelyn watched as her companion flicked through the channels. The screen picture landed like a wheel of fortune on a popular American television drama. As Evelyn lifted her mouth to her wine glass her eyes casually glazed over to the screen where time seemed to stop. It was a surreal moment. There, in front of her, highly defined in medieval costume and complete with a stubbled jaw was Jack King.

Evelyn's friends were none the wiser as they enjoyed the television show on the screen in front of them. They were all new friends of Evelyn's in America. Jack had never been brought up in any topic of conversation, not out loud anyway. In every moment of silence her soul whispered his name as she tried to forget him. In her internal silence, a wash of happiness covered the undercurrent of how much she missed being with him. She was genuinely happy for Jack. A new credit in the most popular show in the world.

# # #

For the days that followed, her mind screamed with his name reverberating around her skull. She desperately pleaded with God to take away the pain in her heart that was chained to his soul. She loved him so much. A close friend talked to her frail figure over a video call, virtually attempting to cradle her, as she wept helplessly.

"He will be the death of you. Come on Evelyn. Please. Just have something to eat. Your scaring us all." Silently, Evelyn looked on, her determination wilted.

# # #

He may have been appearing on screen but Jack was fighting his own personal battles. A small black, solid iron safe sat in front of him, as the dial called for him to open it.

He didn't want this. Debt was mounting and he owed a lot of favors. The quick clicks of the circular safe dial echoed as Jack's hand turned it, unlocking it using the secured combination. Resting inside lay a shining black ex service, Browning Hi Power, handgun. Jack's fingers resting in the silence on the smooth rosewood paneled hand grip. Wrapping it up, he placed it carefully in his rucksack. Closing the safe, he reset the dial and left.

# # #

Evelyn was down to her last one hundred dollars with a week left before her rent was due. Overdrawn in every account with no access to any cards that didn't decline and having won her last rents money at her first hand in the San Manuel casino, she instinctually knew that this option would not be a reliable source this time around.

It was late and the lights of a gentlemen's club flashed before her as she wandered aimlessly, her mind racing. Two girls exited the back door laughing as they lit up their cigarettes, one of them tending to a tear in her tights as she spoke. Whilst she stopped, the other girl counted a wad of cash. She must have held over three thousand dollars, at least. Evelyn noticing the one hundred dollar bill notes she was counting from her specific spying. The girl quickly hid the money back into her bra as they discussed finding a place to graze after their long shift.

# # #

Jack drove up a long drive leading into a derelict industrial estate near the docklands in East London.

"Where have you been King?"

Jack merely smiled.

"We thought you might've chickened out." A short bald man in a suit with a personalized goatee walked confidently forward.

"I would like to see the money first." Jack spoke firmly, the gun resting in the back of his trousers so as to keep his hands free and his posture deceptively open. Loud, slow water drips pinged onto a nearby acoustic surface from an over head pipe that leaked as it fell from the great height of the warehouse ceiling on the other side of the desolate tin like space.

"Follow me," the shorter man instructed.

# # #

The girls from the Gentleman's Club crossed the road as Evelyn came into view. "You okay, girl?"

"Me?" Evelyn questioned.

"Well unless you think we would talk to him, then yes." The girls gestured to a unwashed hairy homeless man snoring from the sidewalk across the street. They were a similar age to Evelyn, one a bit older perhaps and the other probably slightly younger or that's what their dress code indicated.

"Yes, I'm okay, thank you," she replied.

"You're from England!" Their excitement radiated and as if they were now meeting her royal highness in person and began strangely adjusting their clothing accordingly. Evelyn stood watching their bizarre behavior until they stopped. One of them suggested she should grab a coffee with them. She had nothing else to do. Escaping her money solving mind may have been just what she needed to manifest a coherent answer.

# # #

Jack followed the short man through the maze of the empty warehouse. The wind whistling through its shell as they walked. They came to a door of an unmarked office where the ugly looking man had made himself at home.

"Cup of tea?"

Jack wanted to shoot this waste of space right there and then, his mind games riling him right up. "No thanks, mate." Jack smiled again as the man took his time to make himself one. "You were lucky with the electrics" Jack jested, his patience wearing thin. "So how long do you anticipate this taking?" Jack questioned.

"As long as it takes." The man's only reply.

# # #

Evelyn sat with her two new associates in the booth of a typical American diner. A container of sauces sticky at one end with white napkins which wrapped silver cutlery sat at the ready.

"I'll get these," the older girl offered. "Three house coffees, please."

Before the waitress returned with the coffees, Evelyn said something she couldn't even begin to imagine would leave her mouth. "Is there any work available at your place?"

# # #

Jack sat watching the stout Italian looking man drinking his tea in silence. The slurping becoming excruciatingly painful to his acute ear. Twenty minutes of slurp interrupted silences later, the man spoke, looking up at a round, school-like clock he had wedged above the doorway.

"They'll be here any minute."

# # #

"You want to work with us?" The girls giggled. "You would be awesome. Do you know how much American men would pay for a bit more than a dance with an English woman!" The weight of her words began to dawn on her as she theorized what she had proposed.

# # #

The sound of an arriving car's wheels connecting to the broken tarmac instigated Jack to retrieve the gun tucked in the back of his trousers by his belt loop.

"Do not shoot him until I say," the Italian man demanded.

"I want to see my money before I do anything," Jack stated in a slow, but stern voice.

"There you go wise guy. Let's go." The man unlocked a desk drawer in his office, opening it enough so that Jack could identify the piles of cash awaiting him once the job was complete.

# # #

Chapter 36

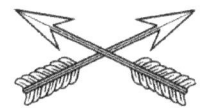

Evelyn rose from the table, flustered at her own question. "Hey, honey, take my number," one of the girls called over as Evelyn began to make for the diner door apologetically. The girl handed her a cute pink business card.

"Thanks," she smiled pleasantly as she took the card and then walked on, the diner door swinging behind her.

# # #

Three men pushed a fourth, silent man into the middle of the main warehouse room. His face was covered with a light brown hessian sack stained with his blood. Hands tied mercilessly behind his back, his wrists raw. The Italian man quizzed him on the location of his alibi. In his refusal to answer the questions asked of him, Jack was instructed to hold the gun to the man's head. He placed the barrel in contact with his skull.

# # #

Evelyn made her way to her car. The girl's card in the pocket of her skinny jeans as she turned the key in the ignition and raced home.

# # #

The victimised man was not giving in to the pressure around him, Jack's gun pressed firmly into his now bowed head. "Pull the trigger." Jack was instructed. He had been in a lot of trouble, but he had never killed a man. Although he was more than capable of doing it with his bare hands and was not unfamiliar with pools of blood. The fist fights may not have left the other party with the ability to walk but they had never died.

"If I am going to do this I am not going to be as cowardly as you lot," Jack announced. Untying the string from the hessian bag, the victim's eyes were sore and swollen as Jack moved around to face him, the pit of his stomach turning.

Waves of doubt began building inside of Jack's worrying gut. He took hold of them firmly in his mind and decided he must focus solely on the task in front of him. To mask his increasing fear Jack began to overcompensate as he boldly confronted the man before him: "I want you to die knowing who killed you."

The victim sat shaking, his bruised eyes just making out the contours of Jack's face as he saw him raise the gun to his forehead. The man was barely conscious as the last touch he yearned to feel was his wife's lips on his. The cold metal from the pistol's barrel was pressed against his pale skull. The front sight on the end of the gun shoved carelessly into his bloodshed forehead. A single resounding shot from the gun penetrated the man's forehead as the stained sack lay at his feet.

A silence reverberated through the warehouse briefly before Jack walked immediately to the back room office prizing open the cash draw in anger. He collected more than his money's worth and left wiping his face from the spits of blood that had spat back at him from the shot.

# # #

On the other side of the Atlantic, Evelyn lay motionless in bed, the white business card twiddling between her index finger and thumb. The darkness collided with the stillness of the world outside. The card fell from her grip as she closed her weary eyes and fell asleep, her mind busying as she slept.

The next day washed past, both Evelyn and Jack wondering where to go from here. They dozed separately and helplessly contemplated the evening previous. Today was a long day. Jack's day drew to a near close before Evelyn's whose time zone was eight hours behind his.

The following evening approached and Evelyn decided action must be taken. She drove to the club where she had met the girls the night before. The broad shouldered doormen eyed her up as she walked down the red carpeted staircase and through the leather cushioned double doors. Music blared as her eyes landed on a toned woman in her bra and knickers dancing for a suited gentleman enjoying his private show. Evelyn sat at the bar, looking and feeling very out of place.

"A double rum and coke, please," she politely asked the bartender who greeted her with a smile. The attractive woman working at the bar became intrigued with

Evelyn's spirit and took a moment to continue her curiosity eyeing her up and down, her eyes affecting Evelyn's comfortability in the chair.

"I'll bring it over."

"Ok," Evelyn's innocence prevailing in her short reply.

The bartender was slender in her appearance, her long brown hair resting in front of her on the front of her slightly open shirt. Pouring the drink she kept a firm eye on Evelyn with prying eyes.

Evelyn was out of her depth, resting back in her chair, longing for the arrival of her drink. The bartender positioned a short black spirit straw in Evelyn's drink with care placing it on a tray and carrying it over to Evelyn.

"You waiting for a dance honey?"

"Me? No. No, not at all."

"Why are you down here then?" The woman's questions became suddenly very intrusive as Evelyn sipped her drink in a silent response. Looking down into her own lap to avoid eye contact with the bar staff, Evelyn slowly realised the woman was hitting on her. "What are you doing later? I get off at 2 a.m. if you fancy a drink somewhere else."

"Um, I don't think so. Thank you, though."

"Suit yourself, you look like you need loosening up but if your not interested in trying something new I get it." She walked back towards the bar. "How do you know you don't like something if you have never tried it?" she continued teasingly.

Evelyn relaxed into the banter. "How do you know I have never tried it?" Evelyn sparred. Sipping her drink

Evelyn knew she had to leave. The ice sat alone in the glass and she exited the same way she entered, puzzling the staff who watched her leave.

# # #

Chapter 37

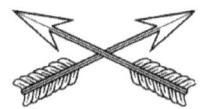

Lost, but hopeful of the next miracle, she had come to realize that God was on her side. Fighting back the tears, she struggled to have coffee with a friend and later a dinner with a wise mentor opened the flood gates of her frustration. Battling with the justifications of her negative ego, Evelyn became overwhelmed. That night Evelyn fell exhausted into an unusually deep sleep.

Scuffing her feet, head up, determined like a modern viking, she returned to her favorite coffee shop to renew her plans. The communal resting place was assorted with colourful yet faded donated furniture, an arty feel with a small stage space for poets and musicians. The old bookcase resonating like a welcoming public library for the customers that indulged in their freshly roasted coffee and homemade gluten free cakes and cookies.

An instant message conversation with her mum played on her iphone, the tears filling her eyes once more as she placed her dark Ray Ban sunglasses on inside to disguise her pain. To the right of her, two young guys worked tirelessly on what looked like a script, the occasional banter spurring each other on.

Evelyn opening her really retro macbook laptop took a deep breath and selected a new blank document. The battery icon in the top right hand corner of the screen turned red. "Great."

She searched through her black laptop holdall for a power cord with a UK plug, remembering the adaptor remained at home. Looking up, she noticed one of the guys had a Mac and a charger, and politely asked if she could use it. A conversation begun which led to Evelyn curiously asking about the project they were writing. A novel, they replied.

The novelists' friend left soon after leaving its writer and Evelyn alone. As Evelyn became more intrigued, the young man recalled his process in reaching his publishing deal. Evelyn had already started her own novel, a story close to her heart but was fearful to reveal it. With nothing to lose she followed his instructions carefully.

A much need trip home to England was nearing. This trip home she had to tell Jack how she felt. Her silence in her own feelings were eating her up. She had urged Jack to communicate clearly with her in the past but upon looking back Evelyn noticed she was the one who had never once told him how she had really felt.

She had braved living alone in another country, fighting her own battles in life. It was time, and upon her return she would contact Jack. This time she would step up and face the ultimate fear, conveying to him her honest feelings. She wanted to ask him to come back to L.A. with her.

# # #

Chapter 38

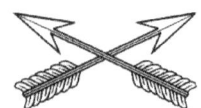

Jack hadn't worked as an actor for seven months and was tirelessly auditioning with no results, coming to the decision that perhaps it wasn't going to work out for him. A numbness prevailed around a name. Evelyn Wise.

His love life was looking positive on the surface and with Evelyn out of sight he had physically moved on. He made plans to love unconditionally and would commit himself fully to someone else.

Evelyn returned to England for a couple of months to visit her family and friends, signing with a new agent in England. It wasn't in her plan to meet Jack so soon, but her heart longed for him and a hand written letter was sent. He responded immediately agreeing to see her, his heart racing as he groomed himself for the occasion.

It had been over a year and a half since they had been united. The longest amount of time for which they had not seen each other since they first met. Both of them had convinced themselves that no matter what they felt for each other, however powerful, they were perhaps not destined to be together.

Evelyn had not missed a day where she had not thought of Jack. In every moment of inner solitude, Jack's intuition had whispered Evelyn's name. A meeting with Woody Allen would have caused less nervousness in comparison to how they had felt this morning.

The sun shone on the two houses. He showered with integrity. She shampooed with spirit. The meeting approached.

Dialing the once familiar number, Jack took a deep breath before pressing the button to connect the call. Evelyn locked her apartment door behind her and walked casually outside to meet him as he called her to tell her he had arrived.

She had told him to wait outside the apartment, but he was now unsure which one was hers. Upon seeing her, he reversed nervously like a boy racer backing up to where Evelyn stood waiting, avoiding the oncoming car as it swerved out of his way. The stranger was surprised and somewhat enraged by Jack's unexpected and careless driving. Having always loved the car model of Mercedes he was now driving a new black compact Mini Cooper. His large frame compacted into the vehicle. The change of car was certainly the influence of another woman. Evelyn smiled, his driving hadn't changed. Their eyes met, as Jack instructed his car window to lower. So much had happened for both of them.

She looked different, more mature, more like a woman than the girl he had originally met. Her blonde hair now long and dark and flowing behind her smart black suit jacket. Unbeknownst to Evelyn, her appearance was not too dissimilar to another woman in Jack's life.

Evelyn took him in. He had finally sorted out his appearance, exchanging his tie-dyed linen trousers for jeans and black boots. He now looked like he had walked out of an All Saints store rather than a charity shop, although previously vowing he never wanted to follow the crowd. This revamped style was most definitely influenced from someone else.

They talked freely, the conversation picking up as if they had never been apart. They were most definitely kindred spirits. Taking each other in, their energy radiating towards each other. They stopped for a coffee as they drove towards a country pub for lunch that Jack had selected for the reunion.

Parking in the woodland car park opposite the restaurant, Jack insisted a walk was in order to build up an appetite. Evelyn was wearing heels in preparation for a meeting she would be attending later that day. Rooting in the boot of the car, Jack fetched her some flip flops -- a women's pair. Curiously Evelyn tried them on, her gut reacting.

"Who's are these?" Evelyn asked outright.

"Sarah's," he lied.

Evelyn knew Sarah was his sister. She also knew they weren't hers. It would have been highly unlikely for her to have flip flops in her brother's car in the winter months, not with the cold English climate.

Without a coat, Jack wrapped Evelyn up in his hooded jumper as they set off into the woodlands. The sun's glares shimmered through the trees as they strolled. Evelyn wasn't entirely sure whether it had been planned but this was the same woodlands they had been to on their famous run up Heartbreak Hill which she had conquered in an effort not to have hers broken. They walked further into the woods alone, away from any sign of civilization.

They strolled side by side. The energy radiating between the kindred spirits. Jack began the conversation with enthusiasm telling a story he hoped would impress her. As he continued, Evelyn watched as he began waving his hands with descriptions of his tale. As she listened, enthralled by the words he spoke, Evelyn glanced over noticing something wholly unfamiliar. A gold ring on his fourth finger reflected into her eyes from the sunlight that flickered through the tall trees. The luscious green leaves swirled in the sunlight, blurring her vision as Jack's hand and the newly placed circle of gold seemed to dance in front of her.

# # #

Chapter 39

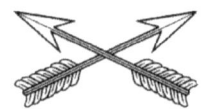

Her legs continued to move as her whole world stood still. She double checked to see which hand he wore it on by consulting her own and then rechecking again.

Evelyn quietly prayed her fears would be cancelled out as she longed to see the religious symbol placed on his right hand and not left. The ring continued to glisten in the sunlight as they walked on through the woodlands.

It was on his left hand. His wedding finger.

Looking at the soiled earth below her, Evelyn wished it would open and swallow her up. Two words struggled and finally reached her bitten bottom lip.

"What's that?" she asked, interrupting his tale and pointing to his hand.

"Oh yer, yer...," Jack stumbled in return.

Minimizing the situation by attempting to not make it important. Silence sat in the next sixty seconds. Jack questioned why he hadn't said anything to her before now. It wasn't the best way for her to find out, he knew that. He had had plenty of opportunities. It was never going to be an ideal time. At least it wasn't through anyone else, over a text or the phone he cowardly told himself.

He was getting older now and his needs weren't being met. He wanted a purpose, someone to love and cherish him. A family to provide for.

Evelyn was internally crushed. Why had he never told her about this? Jack wondered what was he suppose to say? The next words formed his reply. "It wasn't planned... it just sort of happened," he stumbled trying to find the right words to stable both of them.

He continued with a spring in his step and a wholly irrelevant story. "Strange really, my best friend, you know the one that looks like William Dafoe? He did it at the same time, unbeknown to me."

It was a rather odd response as he began playing the engagement down enormously. "I was drunk and we were having a cocktail and I just asked her."

The sound was a blur, a dream, a haze of sounds merging together as her mind frantically tried to make sense of it all and react coherently. Surprising herself, the direct opposite reaction to how she was feeling sprung excitedly from her mouth.

"Congratulations, that's amazing news! I am so happy for you!" she proclaimed with genuine happiness, a sickness sitting in the pit of her stomach. So many questions pained her thoughts as they continued their conversation as if this catastrophic event wasn't a part of their reality.

Jack had been dreading this moment. He had quite honestly thought he may never see Evelyn again. This strained conversation was difficult for him too.

The sunlight poured through the canopy of green leaves above them. Jack wondered what would happen if society had no rules. How would they behave right now? What they would say?

It was amazing to Evelyn how strategically they had skirted around the only real thing that needed discussing. They covered every other area including their past relationship in intricate details. Memories of hauntingly loving things they use to do, events they had experienced together, both of them recalling things they never thought the other would have remembered.

I still love you and probably always will leaving both of their lips coated in a distant but happy grieving energy. They were like a drug to one another--their time together being their fix.

They were addicts who had been good by not surrendering to its persistence over the years but climbing the walls as the lack of it penetrated their hearts daily. Whilst continuing to discuss events of the past with him, her mind swam hurriedly through her confused thoughts wondering when this had happened, why he had never told her, what she was doing whilst he was waiting at the aisle for someone else to walk down it?

Had this been going on for years; were they together when Evelyn was seeing Jack? Were their children involved? She wanted to vomit. Her stomach turned at the very thought of it all. He was married to someone else. He had proposed and married someone else.

This wasn't a girlfriend; this was a wife, a life long commitment until death do us part. And still, she was smiling back at him, positive, upbeat, undeterred by this bombshell he had thrown at her without the decency to previously mention.

Why hadn't he told her? Was he truly happy? Did he ever think of marrying her? The stories circulated until her head pounded as muddy as the squelching under her feet, filthy in now what must have been his wife's flip flops.

# # #

Chapter 40

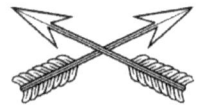

Kicking off the flip flops into what Evelyn now questioned could have been his wife's car too, Evelyn's muddied toes thankfully reentered her own shoes. In the back of the car, Evelyn chose to ignore the child's scooter sprawled across the back seats as she continued to wish the world would swallow her whole.

They crossed the puddles from the rurally fenced car park to the pub. Evelyn's whole body screamed 'don't marry her, marry me.' But her pride stopped her from making a fool of herself at the risk of being rejected. The fear stopping her dead. She knew if she had said this and he had rejected her, her heart would never recover. She stupidly suppressed saying anything that might cause upset for him, continuing to suffer as she swallowed her suggestion in the silence.

He didn't know what she was thinking. He didn't want to hurt her. Perhaps he should have mentioned it before, but if she knew, he knew she wouldn't have wanted to meet him. He wanted to see her, it had been so long, too long and he too, had thought of her almost every day, a turmoil of emotions he battled with daily.

He had to move on. She had gone. She was living with someone else in another country, or so he had thought. The jealously of this arrangement she had informed him of burning beneath his surface. He always privately entertained his desires of a life with Evelyn, even now as she smiled at him from the other side of the pub table. He would imagine them in the garden with their children playing make believe games. Her touch in the morning. Making love as the sun rose and they started their day together. Evenings spent chatting about acting, snuggled in front of a movie as they worked towards their collective goals, pinning images on a shared life board of things they would accomplish together.

They laughed over the pub lunch despite their broken hearts they were both bursting with love. So similar in their ways. Determined, successful and motivated, their best intentions always painting the paths of their often overly ambitious plans. Practically they probably needed someone stable to balance their dreams with reality, but it was fun in their world. Their ideal world was not tinged with the cruelties reality held.

They left each other that day with a smile and a friendly hug. So many words were left unsaid. Jack drove thoughtfully, ignoring a call on his mobile from his agent. He would phone her back. His mind was elsewhere.

He stopped in a space of solitude taking off his ring and placing it on the car's dashboard. It was his Grandad's ring. He hadn't got married yet, but wore it to keep his fiancée happy. She was adamant that he should signify he was committed to her and he agreed in order to keep the peace.

# # #

Chapter 41

Parking opposite the ocean Jack reflected on whether he had made the right decision. He needed to be loved. He wanted to be in love. He had dreamt of being loved unconditionally, those lonely days of pain, alone in his empty home were a distant memory and now he did have someone to share it with.

She was a good woman, strong and not needy--yet needing Jack enough to give him a strong sense of purpose. Evelyn would be ok, she was a survivor; she was young. He had never believed she would love him forever anyway. He convinced himself that it was the right decision, against an unsettling feeling in his stomach.

# # #

Evelyn walked from Jack's car to the tube station her mind processing what had happened. It had been quite an unanticipated revelation amongst the afternoon banter. Before allowing her emotions to take over, she sat calmly listening internally to how she really felt.

In all the other unexpected responses that day the whispers in her heart sounded odd. "He had chosen someone else" the words rang in her head. The bitter taste of being second best never had sat well with her.

Evelyn and Jack stayed in shy and polite contact, a new dimension to this relationship attempting to formulate. The words "mate" rolled across messages as if they could ever be. A confused phone call between them also allowed Jack to share the information that he was not married but engaged and the ring was a sign of his commitment.

# # #

London awoke. The crisp autumn sun rising. The trees in the suburbs were loosing their leaves, now carpeting the pavements creating a natural trail of flame colours, the school children walking over them with backpacks high, the seasonal change marking the final term of the year.

Evelyn was staying with a friend for a couple of days as Jack washed his face getting ready for an audition in central London. She parked herself with her laptop in a coffee shop to write. A fresh cup sat at her side the sandlike swirls untouched on the top, the white frothy foam perfect.

# # #

Jack's mobile phone rang as he left the house putting on a warm winter coat closing the front door behind him. His strong strides reached the car in no time and he clambered inside. On his way, he blasted the car with songs from the CD player that got him fired up.

# # #

Evelyn's fingers typed tapping away on her trusty laptop. She was planning her permanent trip back to Los Angeles, methodically calculating expenses.

Evelyn had a meeting with her agent lined up in an hour's time which sat at the forefront of her mind. The city seemed emptier than usual today. Crossing Leicester Square, Evelyn made her way through China Town towards Tottenham Court Road, opting to use Soho as a cut through. The traffic was backing up. A big red double decker bus had wrongly navigated a roundabout causing cabbie chaos.

# # #

Instead of parking in his usual area of perfect parking spots, Jack had to settled for somewhere elsewhere and walk. He walked confidently down Wardour Street as Evelyn elegantly crossed Shaftesbury Avenue, her coat tail blowing happily behind her in the autumn wind.

Singing to themselves content in their own bubbles, minds active, their feet came to a sudden halt on the unexpected arrival of a familiar face up ahead. Perfect white straight teeth revealed themselves behind loving lips, genuinely grateful for this moment of madness. Time stood still as an isolated moment of two hearts talked for a few minutes as tourists navigated around them, before they continued their journeys.

# # #

Chapter 42

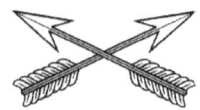

Jack called Evelyn. "I need to see you" his only words.

"What's wrong?"

"We need to talk" he continued.

"Sure, hun." She spoke casually attempting to prompt him for more information.

Jack chucked a bag in his car and headed towards Evelyn's family home. He had never been there before and she was not expecting any visitors today. His mobile phone rang continuously as he drove, the ringing prompting him to accelerate faster down the motorway. For the first time he had not planned what he wanted to say to her.

His adrenaline was racing as he turned off the motorway and down the country lanes to her house until his car entered her driveway. Evelyn now dressed and ready for his arrival, walked to the front door as he rang it. The house was empty. Evelyn kissed him softly on the cheek offering him a drink as he took off his jacket and sat in a state on the sofa. An open fire flickering back at him.

"Evelyn I still love you." Silence echoed through the house. "Say something...," he looked at her, his eyes soft.

"I don't know what to say, Jack," Evelyn composed herself from another emotional upheaval. "So much has happened. I had to accept that you wanted to marry someone else."

"I know," he said hesitantly. "You gave me nothing but love and I pushed you further and further away. The truth is I haven't stopped thinking about you since the day I met you."

The flames flickered in the fire. A pop sounded as another piece of the kindling caught on fire. Evelyn's guard was high. She had let it down too many times before and just because he had changed his mind today she couldn't be sure he wouldn't change it again. After all, he had done so in the past.

"What are you asking me, Jack?"

"I don't know; I'm not sure" he uttered, tears now in his eyes.

"That's just not good enough for me and my heart, I'm afraid." She couldn't back down now.

Jack's phone rang continuously on the passenger seat of his car, his agent wanting to know his whereabouts.

"I am saying this because there is still so much love for you in me and I can't risk giving it all away only for you to take it back later on, deciding you're not sure..." She began listing his past excuses for it not working out before. "The age gap is too big...," she trailed off, sounding heartless, but she had to protect herself.

"Evelyn, I've had more than enough time to think about this. I haven't held you for nearly two years and I still love you. I have never felt like this in my life. Please come and sit with me."

Evelyn walked across the lounge settling at the opposite end of the sofa from Jack. Her big brown eyes hadn't dared look back at his yet. She knew as soon as they fully connected, their individual strengths would weaken. The power of their joint forces were always stronger.

Evelyn raised her eyes catching his. His heart was on his sleeve and she could tell he had meant what he said.

"Please come and sit with me," he repeated.

Evelyn moved along the sofa to him as they lay together. Jack kissed her forehead, stroking her hair and thanking God for this moment. Evelyn's head lay on his heart. The sound of it beating loudly and confirming this was the safest place in the world for her. She surrendered to life for the first time. Their breathing began to become in sync with each other, their gratitude of this moment radiating from them.

"Where do we go from here?" Jack asked.

"Come with me to America" Evelyn announced emphatically.

Jack didn't answer. He needed more time to think about that. Right now he just wanted her at home in his arms.

# # #

Chapter 43

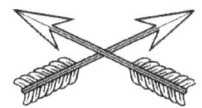

Evelyn's parents were due back soon. To explain who Jack was and why he was here would be no easy task. Exhausted from emotion, Evelyn decided today wouldn't be the best day to start this lengthy explanation.

It was decided that Evelyn would pack a bag and stay with him for a few days. He had not yet moved in with his fiancée, both still leading quite separate lives although they had planned to do things properly in the near future.

Even though they were exhausted, the drive back in his fiancée's Mini to the familiar surroundings of Jack's house proved joyful. Songs were sung in a duet fashion as they collaborated with the professionals singing on the radio. Eventually bored with singing, their hands habitually wandered once more.

He opened the front door of his house for her as she stepped inside. The memories of them entering it so many times before illuminated their souls. The house now looked incredible.

"I took your advice to sort this place out," he smiled.

"It looks great," she responded impressed.

He would give her the tour in the morning. They slipped off their shoes, walking up the now beautifully carpeted cream staircase. After years apart, they lay happily together once more, next to each other on the bed in his newly decorated bedroom.

"I just need to check something..." Evelyn sat up and jumped joyfully off the big bed. She reached the landing in between the bedrooms, walking towards the spare room. Clasping the handle she pulled down on it as it opened out onto the newly painted and varnished white bedroom. The space was cleanly painted with minimalistic features complete with beautiful wooden floors. She smiled turning to face Jack, walking across the hall and falling into his arms with relief.

"I told you I gave it all up when you left," Jack announced. "I cleared this place out. You were right. I have been dying to show you all this." Jack's right hand rested on the left hand side of Evelyn's face as he looked into her loving eyes and kissed her.

Picking her up, Evelyn wrapped her bendy yoga legs around his solid waist as his cold hand rested inside her jumper on her naked, toned back.

Jack lay Evelyn gently down on his bed, her long hair spreading out behind her in the waves of the divine white duvet. He pulled his t-shirt over his head. Evelyn looked up at him as his cold hands gripped her around her waist easing her jumper up, stopping to enjoy her breasts in his hands and sneaking them outside her bra whilst kissing her neck.

# # #

A knock came sounded at the front door early the next morning. Waking with their hands still held Jack smiled at Evelyn, his heart so thankful she was beside him once more. The knocking at the front door grew louder. Instinctively, they knew this was the sound of a jealous rage.

"Jack King open this door now!" Jack walked down the stairs as Evelyn pulled on her jeans and Jack's t-shirt. Jack's fiancé stood at his front door as Evelyn waited out of sight upstairs.

"Who is she Jack?"

Jack stood in silence. The woman's eyes filling with tears.

"Please, Jack," she pleaded softly.

Evelyn waited cautiously at the top of the stairs. She didn't want to hurt anyone, but she loved Jack. The silence continued as Jack's blue eyes looked at the woman in front of him.

"She's everything," Jack stated. His fiancé's eyes streamed with tears rushing down her fair cheeks.

Jack's heart was torn. Evelyn certainly had a pull on his heart, but he had told himself so many times that they could never be. His head was spinning, every time he closed his eyes he saw Evelyn's face. She was a secret in his heart. The only time she was mentioned was when his lips were unable to keep quiet any longer, her name spilling from his lips to a friend over a coffee, an excuse to say it.

His heart had yearned to hear from her whilst she had been in America but life had taken its toll and had carried him with the social current; he had moved on. His future decisions were now in front of him crumbling.

"Jack, please," she repeated. "What is going on?"

"I don't want to hurt you." he confessed.

"Stay here if you want but I need to go for a walk." Jack whistled for his dog as his fiancé got back in her car as he knew she would and drove off infuriated.

Evelyn made her way to the kitchen, pressing the plastic black button down on the kettle to instruct it to boil. The sound of the kettle heating rattled in the deafening filled silence. Sitting at the wooden table Evelyn grappled with her self respect. As of yet not a word had left her lips and she had not seen this woman.

# # #

He walked through the long grass, his stout dog bounding at his side, unaware of his owner's turmoil. Jack tried to calm his thoughts willing his intuition to whisper an answer. Reaching the water's edge he spoke out loud. A prevalent discussion with God, he would know what to do.

The sea air gathered as a black cloud broadened overhead and the sunlight faded in misery. Jack knew a storm approaching when he saw one. He turned back without his answer, heading home as the raincloud began to empty, spitting at first before the heavens opened.

His trainers springing off marshland grass and around muddy puddles that settled in the potholes on the trodden dirt track. Bigger droplets of rain were now pounding down onto the shimmering black sea. Without an umbrella, Jack arrived back at his house, his thick short dark hair dripping from the unexpected shower.

Evelyn had to leave; he wanted to be on his own.

# # #

Chapter 44

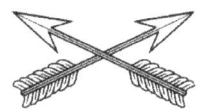

"We're born alone, we live alone, we die alone. Only through our love... can we create the illusion for the moment that we are not alone." Evelyn sat in her kitchen, reading one of her favorite quotes from Orson Welles. She wanted to make sense of it all.

She was still bemused that Jack wore a wedding ring -- a symbol that he was actually married and not just engaged. The questions she had wanted to ask had not been raised in this fleeting affair.

A message was sent and Jack replied immediately asking if everything was ok. He offered to come and see her, but her heart and pride were determined that a tear would not be shed in his presence and right now her soul was yearning to emote. She didn't have the strength left to say what she wanted to, without the vulnerability to wear her heart on her sleeve, perhaps her greatest downfall. Their conversation took place on the telephone.

In the conversation Jack revealed he wore his ring to display his commitment. Jack never apologised for hurting Evelyn, the sorry rule from his handbook ingrained habitually. He continued by discussing their past sex life and his enjoyment of it.

Evelyn was quite sure his fiancé wouldn't be too happy to hear him discussing this topic. Jack finished the conversation by adding that if he wasn't with the woman he was with, he probably would be with Evelyn, listing all the qualities he loved about her. He recalled specific details and events from their time together.

Evelyn asked him to stop saying such things. She wanted to black out any pinholes of a future and this ounce of hope that remained between them. The conversation came to a close as they agreed they would remain friends, both of their hearts unable to draw a line under it.

# # #

Jack's life was becoming quite domestic as he busied himself with the list of jobs she had written down for him, in preparation for their first "family" Christmas. He sung show tunes to himself from the top of the wooden ladder as he hung the twinkling white lights that would fringe the front porch of their now family home.

# # #

It was Evelyn's favorite Christmas event of the year and after inviting her mum and best friend, who were unfortunately unable to make the date, Evelyn still had a spare ticket to this wonderful annual occasion.

Evelyn's mind wandered towards Jack, her new "friend." In their previous conversations Evelyn had discussed an up and coming Christmas event at the monumental Royal Albert Hall in Kensington, London.

Evelyn enjoyed his company and they always did laugh a lot...perhaps they could be friends. She longed to see him. A casual invitation was sent and quickly Jack replied confirming that of course he would escort Evelyn to this festive Christmas occasion.

Messages were exchanged in the lead up to the event. With the celebration nearing, Evelyn phoned Jack on his mobile. As she did so, she noticed that the dial tone was unusual, it sounded like it was connecting to a phone that was currently abroad. Jack answered promptly. "Hello...who's that?"

"Me," Evelyn answered. She knew he knew it was her.

"Who's me?"

Evelyn played along with his infuriating game, knowing that he was doing it for the benefit for someone else in the room, most obviously his fiancée.

Jack described that he was on holiday. He had never been away since she had known him, only to work, and so this trip seemed surprising. Evelyn gauged her inappropriate timing to talk as the brief conversation was ended by her encouraging him to enjoy his trip.

On his return, Jack and Evelyn conversed about the up and coming concert. In it Jack discussed that his agent, upon hearing about the event, wanted to go too.

A shared friend whom Evelyn and Jack knew, Robert Taylor, was also going to the event and because she had a spare ticket, she invited herself as his guest. Evelyn knew of their agent from the industry, mainly through Jack. Now all four of them would be there to share the occasion together and Jack announced to Evelyn that he was very much looking forward to it.

The evening arrived and The Royal Albert Hall was suitably decorated for a distinguished Christmas affair. The gigantic real Christmas tree took pride of place upstage. Its grandiose appearance dressed in elaborately expensive tinsel trimmings and colourful lights. The historic venue housed the happy memories of thousands of people who had graced its doors across the decades.

In advance of this evening's proceedings, a row of formal looking empty chairs were arranged sharply upon the stage. Lined with military precision, they awaited an exquisitely dressed choir of children who were readying themselves backstage for this momentous occasion.

Towards stage left, an assortment of music stands awaited the orchestra. Professional trumpeters shined their brass instruments in anticipation of the annual festive melodies in which they would shortly recite.

Evelyn tried to attend this particular event every year and was excited by the spirit of Christmas that she knew this evening would bring. She hadn't told a soul she had invited Jack. She knew in her heart of hearts she shouldn't have, but she couldn't help looking forward to seeing him.

Jack King prepared himself for this evening's event, nervously wondering whether going tonight was the right thing to do. A crisp black buttoned shirt and long legged suit trousers hung neatly on a hanger on the back of his bedroom door as his black socked feet and his bare legs padded across the carpeted floor.

Dressing himself smartly, he threaded his black leather belt through the belt loops of his trousers and took a step back from the long mirror on his bedroom wall. He was a lot older than Evelyn, but prided himself on his not so bad looks for his age.

Jack grabbed a bottle of water and some healthy snacks for the journey. Turning the key in his car's ignition he set off to meet Evelyn at her hotel. Evelyn had arrived at her hotel room as she unpacked a small travel suitcase housing her things for this evening's stay. Evelyn washed happily in the shower, her long wet hair dripping as the water rushed down her back and onto her naked legs before reaching the base of the shower floor. As she dried herself Evelyn noticed that her actions spoke louder than the thoughts she had told herself. She knew Jack and she could never be friends because she still loved him.

# # #

Chapter 45

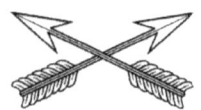

Evelyn and Jack had come to know a lot of people from their time in the industry. One of Evelyn's friends was a radio DJ on one of the major channels across London. With the station now worldwide, Evelyn tuned in to his show on a small television in the hotel suite. On the off chance he might say hello on air, she messaged him. He wished Jack and Evelyn a fantastic night as Jack enjoyed Evelyn's requested personal announcement across the capital on his journey in the car to meet her.

After a two-hour car journey from his house, Jack parked and texted Evelyn's mobile number as he rested in the driver's seat waiting to find out which hotel room she was in. Brushing himself down, he exited the car, checking his appearance in the car's wing mirror while popping a mint in his mouth as he went. Jack locked the car behind him and headed for the hotel entrance.

# # #

The Copthorpe Tara hotel resided in the royal borough of Kensington and Chelsea. A stone's throw away from the popular London locations of Knightsbridge and Notting Hill. From the outside, the hotel resembled more of a large London hospital than a hotel. It was an older building, but not old enough, to boast itself as a classical piece of architecture. It had missed out on the intricate details that its neighbouring buildings pertained.

In its day it would have been exceptionally modern. Its glass cuboid criss-crossed white front undoubtedly had once been the envy of the other aging structures in London, but today it was by no means timeless. The hotel housed eight hundred and thirty three guest rooms, cleanly kept and quite magically decorated inside. The interior design was classical and typically English in all its features except the staff who were a collection of professionals from all over the world.

Jack's heart raced as he walked through the revolving glass doors of the four star hotel, questioning his feelings as he went. A large oak reception area greeted him on his arrival. The cream marble floors creeping up toward tall pillars, which continued on to the broad white ceilings. The reception staff smiled at him invitingly as he located the lifts.

Jack still turned heads, his tall muscular structure and strong jaw were complimented by the sharp black designer suit that was tailored to his toned physique. His appearance this evening was fairly plain in its colour scheme: black shirt, black shoes, black trousers and a black jacket. The only splash of colour was a new ring gleaming from his tanned hand. The old one marked the commitment. This one would confirm Evelyn's fear.

An official gold band wrapped snugly around his fourth finger on his left hand. Since he had last seen

Evelyn he had shortened the engagement period to his fiancée by actually getting married. He naturally had informed everyone in the world...except Evelyn.

# # #

Chapter 46

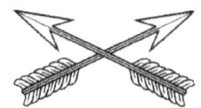

Jack entered the lift from the hotel lobby, memories of his times with Evelyn flooding back. He had tracked her every move this year. He knew everything she had posted via social media and so did the woman he had married.

Jack's wife was nervous about tonight. He had told her that he was meeting his friend, Evelyn. Their history, he decided to omit. The tale he told selected specific information yet diverted his wife from suspecting anything near the truth. The fact that he had had the best sex of his life with Evelyn remained secret. His primitive instincts yearned at the thought.

Jack was interrupted from his sexual fantasies as the lift announced its arrival on the eleventh floor. Jack counted the rooms leading up to Evelyn's along the hall. He followed the signs that labelled Evelyn's room in the groups of hotel rooms that were separated along different sections of the spacious top floor of the building. A large black hotel suite door numbered one hundred and nineteen announced that he had reached his desired destination. His heart raced as he stood tall, knowing that Evelyn was close. Jack knocked confidently.

Readying herself, equally nervous, she headed for the door to greet him. A pause breathed between the two of them.

"Room Service!" he joked, smiling at her as she opened the door to him.

Jack was taken aback as Evelyn stood elegantly in a long, black evening dress. Her brown hair placed in front of her shoulders, the expensive dress hugging indulgently to her slim figure. He had never seen her dressed up quite like this before and began to recollect the innocence and femininity he had fallen for years ago.

Jack complimented her extensively, his nerves high. Unrehearsed words flowed cooly.

"I didn't wear a tie" he commented. "I thought it would be safer, just in case you tried to strangle me later; I know what you're like," he said softly teasing Evelyn.

The room was quiet and softly lit. The lamps attached to the sides of the double bed creating the only light alongside the those from the world outside which twinkled from the window. Two large grandfather type armchairs also lived at that edge of the room with a small wooden table that Evelyn had placed some snacks she had picked up earlier.

Jack's shiny black shoes passed her shimmering gold heels on the soft hotel room carpet as he made his way across to the other end of the room, placing a soft kiss on her cheek and greeting her properly. Jack stood at the vast window at the other end of the room admiring the view of the city that spanned the width of the hotel suite and Evelyn made her way over, standing by his side.

The Victorian rooftops of Kensington spoke volumes between this moment of silent solitude. The city landscape graced the entire breadth of the horizon. As they looked out, the lights from the windows of strangers offered up a wealth of stories untold. Briefly, they remembered their fun with the video camera and the pants party, years prior.

Their story became the size of a dot as both of them gazed from the room out towards the world. Jack moved to alter his view of the picturesque city and stood behind Evelyn as they identified the vibrant pink lights that marked the top of the London Eye. A chemistry still lingered lightly between them. The magnetism of their hands were held back against their habits, remaining firmly by their own smartly dressed sides. A library of sensual memories were stored tightly in the molecular cells of their bodies. It felt like a lifetime ago since they had held one another.

Looking out towards the romantic town where their love had been planted and grown, the temptation to kiss the back of her neck and whisper in her ear before sliding his hands up the bottom of her dress was overpowering as the hotel made bed loomed in Jack's peripheral vision.

Evelyn wanted to feel him pressed up behind her in his suit trousers as the privacy began proving too much. Reminding himself of his recent committed decision, Jack encouraged them to move and go for a drink in the bar downstairs. Evelyn wondered if they might have torn each other's clothes off if they had stayed a moment longer. With her evening bag collected, they called the lift from the lobby, laughing as they walked side by side down the hallway.

Exiting the classically English elevator, Jack led Evelyn to the polished hotel bar. It was around the opposite corner to the lifts from the hotel reception desk. The bar was generous in size, but smart and well kept. A line of optics were parked along the back wall of the bar, their tempting spirited liquids still in their glass bottles. This evening the bar was fairly empty. A few male hotel guests were enjoying a "business" drink or two at the expense of their company, their ties now loosely confirming they had most definitely finished work for the day.

On their approach Evelyn's appearance caught the eye of a stranger who watched Evelyn and Jack walk in together. The stranger, a fairly large middle aged African American man, rose from his seat and confidently walked towards them. The man approached Jack who was now ordering them drinks from the barman.

"Can I just say your girlfriend is looking extremely gorgeous this evening, sir." Jack and Evelyn laughed nervously, unsure of how to react to this. The man was of course completely unaware of the new friendship dimension that they now attempted to live by. Jack took the reigns and thanked him before completing the ordering of their drinks.

"You just got upgraded," Jack smiled, joking with Evelyn without correcting the kind gentleman and taking the compliment, conveniently forgetting to mention his new wife.

Finding an intimate table away from the other people in the bar, Jack and Evelyn sipped their drinks, Evelyn listening as Jack told his latest story, a tale involving his agent and a man selling the big issue.

Their fondness for each other was captured in their eyes. Their souls speaking another story. The African American man watched on, envious of their love, unaware that what he saw was a relationship that could never be.

The emptiness of Evelyn's glass prompted her to consult the time on her phone. It was nearing the start time of the concert. Jack finished his drink as they headed towards the main reception. The cars were due to arrive any minute to deliver them to the VIP guest entrance where the photographers were waiting. A tall, young male driver, appropriately dressed, greeted them. Complete with white gloves and an equally suitable, black chauffeur's hat, the polite man opened the car door as Jack and Evelyn climbed inside.

The two of them talked continuously in the car often including the driver so that he did not feel like he was left out. Evelyn questioned to herself that everyone probably did that, and he probably would much rather be left to drive than have to endure another round of pleasant small talk, but she continued to talk to him anyway.

Jack and Evelyn discussed the year to date as Jack revealed his honest frustrations about his lack of acting work to Evelyn. She was always easy to talk to. Jack had loved their conversations and missed Evelyn's perspective on things. The smart black car pulled up to the entrance as the driver opened the door for the two of them. Jack got out first, offering his hand to Evelyn.

Standing tall as her eloquent shoes connected to the ground, the driver slowly closed the car door behind them. Standing with the car at their side and the Royal Albert Hall a few feet in front of them, Jack's hand reached for Evelyn's as it had done so many times before and in response she instinctively held it back.

With her hand held safely in his, Jack walked them into the venue. Evelyn was greeted with a warm welcome by a host of familiar faces as she introduced Jack to the charity event organisers. After a short conversation Evelyn was encouraged to have her photo taken by the photographers who were looking after the event.

Evelyn whispered to Jack as their eyes met. "Do you want to join me for the photos?" Evelyn asked cautiously.

"Yes, I would love to, little one," he confirmed as they took to the press board and the lights began to flash. A photographer flashed and mused that they looked perfect together.

# # #

Chapter 47

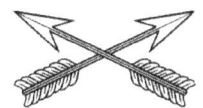

Jack and Evelyn were escorted up in a large grey lift by a kind member of the charity event team. As the lift doors opened they followed the woman who walked them towards the box that they would be watching the Christmas Carol Concert from. As they progressed, their formal shoes took superior strides across the red carpeted hallways, the walls mounted with gold frames. A number of large, black royal looking doors began to appear at the curvature of the left hand side wall which housed the entrance to the royal boxes.

The woman who directed them, slowed her strides as they drifted over to the right, stopping completely at one door in particular. The ceremonial portal was stamped with a white sheet of paper. It listed Evelyn's name with a plus one highlighted amongst the other names that were underneath and they were welcomed in.

The view of the Royal Albert Hall was indeed incredible. The one hundred and eighty degree view of history was a wash of royal red as the seats began to fill with patrons above and below them. The magic of

Christmas racing through the aisles and dusting each chair with love.

The other names on the door began to illuminate themselves as Jack and Evelyn joined their fellow box companions for the evening. The excitement of the event made introductions easy. Male hands shook as Evelyn politely received some more kisses on her cheek. A friend of Evelyn's offered them a glass of champagne, which they received gratefully, enjoying the light bites and nibbles that were laid out on the smartly organised table of food and drink, just inside the door.

Jack made his way to the front of the red velveted interior twelve-seater box to look for his agent, Charlotte, and their friend, Rob. His eyes scanned the overlooking view carefully deciphering if they were in the hundreds of people who were taking their seats. He was keen to find them but was out of luck as the orchestra announced the beginning of the concert. Jack took his seat next to Evelyn in anticipation, smiling at her with gratitude.

# # #

The concert was magnificent. The well spoken compere dressed in a bow tie and tails guided them through the evening's entertainment. He conducted the orchestra effortlessly, introducing several solos that were sung by well-known television faces, several of them friends with Evelyn. The nature of the event made it wholly interactive offering the audience a chance to sing along with the orchestra on numerous occasions. Jack and Evelyn were entertained as they listened to the other's joyful singing efforts picked up in the aural spaces around them.

Resting in between songs, their arms became entwined on the seat arm rest. In attempt to save on the clapping, Evelyn lifted her linked hand up to join Jack's clap which she placed in the middle. A new creation that stirred amusement between them for a song or two.

Jack and Evelyn clapped furiously as the compere announced an intermission. They had very much enjoyed the first half of the concert. During the break the perfect photo opportunity presented itself. Jack took out his iphone and asked another member of the box to take a photo of them both. Jack wrapped his arm around Evelyn. The rest of the box members none the wiser that the two were only friends without identifying Jack's ring. Their happy cheeks pressed towards each other, their smiles radiating, the Christmas setting of the Albert Hall offering a picturesque back drop.

A few snaps were shot on both their phones which they flicked through after, deciding upon which one made them both look good. As they perused the photos on Jack's phone, his pictures slid past the shots of him and Evelyn and unintentionally onto another photo of a small boy.

The boy could only have been no more than two-years-old and wore a sweet expression as he smiled while playing and looking towards the camera. Jack flicked back to their photos without an explanation as they continued their enjoyment of the concert break, collecting their champagne.

After a champagne topped up interval break, the second half raised the bar and took the concert to a new level as the singing got bolder and the smiles were widened climaxing with the finale which proved to be a fun sing-a-long for all. Evelyn particularly enjoyed "Silent Night," with Jack favoring "O Come All Ye Faithful." The repetition of "O come let us adore him" being the only words he knew, which he bellowed to the thousands just for fun.

The cheers were mightier than the years previous and the money raised for the hosting charity had reached a new record as the concert closed and the 5,272 people prepared for their exit. The Christmas season had officially begun. They left merrily, exiting the bitter cold London air with the festive carols warming their hearts.

# # #

Due to their guest status, Evelyn and her plus one, Jack, were invited to a post event that would be held in The Royal Albert Hall Gallery. The Gallery offered a view from the very top of the building, visually setting the scene for the after party. Although she had seen it before, Evelyn was always taken back by its beauty. The box offered a great view but this was something else.

Jack watched her lovingly and found a free open table to rest at as Evelyn walked towards the beautifully displayed champagne tower of glasses. As she walked, Jack watched her, knowing this would be the last time they would be alone. Treasuring this last moment without wanting her to know, Jack sneakily took a picture of Evelyn using the camera on his mobile.

He loved her little ways and he loved the way that, even despite all the heartache, she had invited him here tonight. He loved how much she loved him. He doubted anyone could love him this much. He had made a commitment to someone else and he had promised himself from that day forward he would remain monogamous.

# # #

Chapter 48

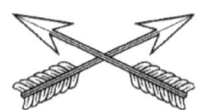

Evelyn turned back around now holding a champagne flute held delicately in her right hand. She saw Jack and realized what he was doing, but smiled nonetheless as she walked back towards him.

The party began to fill up as their friend Rob parted the crowd and said hello to them all. Rob was followed by Charlotte, Jack and Rob's agent. The group gathered around the tall table, enjoying the nibbles that were circulating on trays held by waitresses. The group sipped the complimentary champagne discussing their enjoyment of the evening so far.

Having been the one to introduce Jack all evening, the carpet was swiftly swiped out from under Evelyn's Jimmy Choo shoes as his agent habitually took over in her business like mode.

Charlotte Frank was tall with a strong London accent and knew of Evelyn as an actress in the industry. Charlotte was plain but pleasant looking and she had recently given birth to a baby boy. Evelyn and she had often spoke over email. On one occasion they had discussed possibly working together with the idea of Charlotte representing Evelyn as her agent too. A meeting over coffee that Jack had kindly organised ensued.

Jack stood smiling with the two woman on either side of him and Rob. The conversations bled into each other, the group discussing their not so gifted abilities to carol sing. As the after party numbers increased, a flood of people filled the gallery that ran around the top of the auditorium inside the hall.

Some of these guest visited the table where Jack and Evelyn were seated. The first introduction Charlotte led was directed to two actresses that had wandered over and knew of Charlotte. The woman were dressed in formal evening wear, tipsy with northern accents. With her business head firmly on her shoulders, Charlotte began making introductions around the table, each short and sweet with a name and a brief one word phrase, mainly their job title.

"This is Evelyn Wise; she's an actress. And this is Rob Taylor; he's represented by me..."

The introductory circle finished with Jack, who stood closest to her. Jack's heart skipped a beat and sweat poured across his back. He knew what was coming and he braced himself for the brutal blow. His introduction included a few more words, which gained the attention of Evelyn's ear. "And this is my other half, Jack King."

# # #

Chapter 49

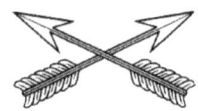

Evelyn's heart felt the piercing of a dagger as the metaphoric knife plunged and tunneled its blade deeper into her already fragile heart. Jack smiled on next to her, beaming obediently from Charlotte's introduction. Evelyn watched Jack stand to attention for Charlotte like a lap dog dumbfounded. Evelyn inwardly questioned through her own positive grin and gritted teeth whether he had ever intended to mention that he had married his agent.

It was something she considered in the back of her mind. Jack was continuously talking about Charlotte but Evelyn never believed he would join the casting couch. The scenario Evelyn had feared in her imagination played out before her very eyes as Charlotte showed off her new trophy. Evelyn's radiant smile was quickly fading from around her cherry glossed lips. The conversation continued for a few moments until Evelyn couldn't keep up her forced positivity any longer. Wanting to throw Jack over the edge of the gallery of The Albert Hall, she politely excused herself.

With her confidence fading, she contained her vulnerability behind a strong posture and painted on smile until she reached the ladies toilets. Having not drunk most of the year, Evelyn was grateful for the alcohol that now raced through her bloodstream. The alcohol mixing meticulously with her adrenaline. Alcohol always had been an effective measure in disguising her pain. Leaving the lavatory cubicle, Evelyn looked at her reflection in the large, ornate mirror that hung luxuriously above the ceramic vanity basins. Her young face emulating the history of their story behind her brown eyes and the windows of her weathered soul.

# # #

Jack chatted with Charlotte and the others as his eyes darted with speed to locate Evelyn. The withheld information had been shared even though in that moment he knew it should have been his lips and not Charlotte's to deliver the news to Evelyn. He knew he should have warned Evelyn. He tried to in the theatre box, but his words failed him and he found himself settling for the unheroic and cowardly option.

He had to find her, but leaving his wife's side to look for Evelyn, who had most certainly left to go to the toilet, would of course arise suspicion. Charlotte sensed his attention wandering away and she took Jack's hand, her fingers securely in between his as he closed his grip cementing their union. Jack's mind darted back to Evelyn's whereabouts. He knew as strong as she was, the moment those labeling words left Charlotte's lips, Evelyn's ever-loving and loyal heart would be crushed.

# # #

Chapter 50

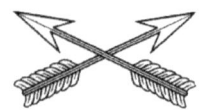

Evelyn returned to the table now controlled and composed only to find Charlotte describing a story of Jack messing around in bed with her. A numbness prevailed as Evelyn's soul stepped outside of herself and she watched on as a humiliated observer. It was most definitely time to leave--this time, for good. Evelyn found the strength to tell Jack that she was leaving. In hindsight, it should have been Jack and Charlotte to leave.

Evelyn was unable to face the others and say goodbye; she just wanted to go. This was the final straw for her. In pain covered by a soft smile, Evelyn left the gallery of the Royal Albert Hall gracefully.

Jack made out he was surprised by her sudden departure. "You're leaving already? Well, it was nice to see you."

His smug remark angered Evelyn. They hugged for the benefit of onlookers. Jack squeezed her tight, noticing the action was not reciprocated. It was confirmation that her love for him had died and he knew in his gut that he would never hear from Evelyn again. She was hurt and his miscommunication had caused her pain.

A number of friendly faces smiled at Evelyn as she mustered up the courage to tell the event organisers she was leaving. A lump the size of a golf ball in her throat kept her goodbyes to a minimum. Her other acquaintances would not realise she had exited the event for the evening. She didn't have the courage to retain a brave face much longer.

# # #

Dressed in a shirt and suit trousers, Rob Taylor was waiting at the exit when Evelyn appeared. He was talking to another group of friends when he noticed Evelyn leaving hurriedly in spite of the night still being young.

Evelyn looked over at him inquisitively. The eye contact between them confirmed that he, too, had known of Jack and Charlotte's plan. An overwhelming sense of betrayal set inside Evelyn.

# # #

Jack barely acknowledged Evelyn's exit, without even an offer to walk her to the awaiting car that would whisk her back to the hotel.

"Well played," Evelyn thought as she left the building. Karma for orchestrating the sly strategy and pulling such a stunt would surely prevail.

Her head was spinning as the missing pieces of the puzzle formulated in Evelyn's racing mind. Her stomach felt sick as she left the venue alone and returned to the hotel in the taxi. The missing links began matching up as the car splashed through the potholed puddles.

Evelyn began understanding Jack's whereabouts on the occasions when he wasn't with her. The international phone call the other week marked the day of their wedding. Had she intuitively felt it and phoned on the day they had married?

Evelyn had expressed her desire to get married on the beach to Jack many times. Had Jack thought of her at all that day? Evelyn questioned whether Charlotte had known how Jack and she met. Surely, she hadn't been in on all this too?

Evelyn was quite sure he wouldn't have spilled every detail to Charlotte. It now seemed plausible that at some point he had been seeing them both. Evelyn began to understand the dramatic over emphasis of the word "mate" that stained their conversations since she had arrived back from Los Angeles...all for Charlotte's benefit.

The combined intelligence of both of these powerful woman had now been played by a man who had not even finished school. They had both known it all deep down, but it was a choice. A choice to live with the disillusioned lies they were fed.

# # #

The walk from the taxi to her room felt like she was wading through water. The need to be alone and release the emotion housed inside of her was overwhelming. As Evelyn opened her hotel room suite, placing her bag on the wooden side by the television, an unfamiliar sense of relief washed over her.

She expected herself to cry. Sitting up in the centre of the bed, a flurry of past instances with Jack revealed themselves in her mind. Memories rewound and a number of warning flags from previous years returned to Evelyn's busy mind.

She recollected his continual reference to Charlotte and recalled her original suspicions, even detailing them to a close friend years earlier. The announcement of dinners with Charlotte, the detail of Charlotte's children, leaving early in the morning, not staying the night unless Evelyn had stayed at his place, the warning from Harry at her party, his leading roles in Charlotte's produced projects. The images continued to circulate.

Evelyn remembered Jack's poignant conversation where he continually emphasized how lucky Evelyn was to not have any baggage. She now figured it was a reference to Charlotte's previous marriage and children, and the myths continued to unravel.

It would seem giving him his freedom had only allowed the opportunity for another woman to take it. Charlotte had him now because Jack needed her. From an outside perspective he was nothing without her.

He had needed Charlotte for work, but now he was trapped. He was unable to move up through the agencies and had been convinced into thinking that America would simply land in his lap without taking any meetings.

He never did have much intelligence Evelyn thought. And yet, the anger had not yet overtaken the ounce of love that still lingered. Would it die when she reflected on what he could have become?

She recalled his fateful words uttered in the taxi. He told her that he would give up if his next project didn't take off. It was due out the following year and she wondered if that too would prove to be a lie.

# # #

Jack and Charlotte enjoyed the rest of their free evening from the Gallery at the top of the Royal Albert Hall. They enjoyed making the most of their time without the kids. As the evening came to a close they used Evelyn's name to secure a free lift back to the hotel. Unbeknownst to Evelyn, Charlotte had booked a suite at the same hotel.

Resting his head beside Charlotte's, Jack took a moment to consider Evelyn before closing his blue eyes. The memories flashed before him as he slept. Evelyn's smile became crystal clear in his mind as her face fore-fronted his thoughts. Jack's heart was heavy as he realised that this chapter was over. Rolling over he kissed his wife goodnight.

# # #

Chapter 51

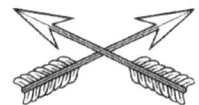

One year later...

A brand new book proudly adorned the desk in an expensively sleek and modern office in Covent Garden. The book's spine was smart and strong. The front cover already made it look like a best seller. All that was missing was an award sticker and a spot on the shelves of the best bookstores around the world.

Snowflakes covered the weathered windowsill, its white paint peeling, the shavings adding to the snowy effect. Beside the book, papers were being organised by a pair of hardworking hands that placed a handwritten letter into a crisp envelope and laid it within the front cover.

The envelope of this letter would later form a memorable bookmark for the recipient who would read the book in rapture. With this envelope now safely tucked inside, the book was wrapped in brown paper and the gift was tied with a plain, white string. The stamped parcel awaited its collection from a bright red Royal Mail van.

#

Jack King shoveled the snow from his driveway in preparation of his family's arrival on this Christmas afternoon.

It was his first Christmas back in his house. In fact, it was the first week back since renting it out for the past two years--an idea Evelyn had suggested to make some money and retire from his criminal activities. Charlotte would lie where Evelyn had slept by Jack's side for the first official time tonight.

Jack continued shoveling as his dog rolled in the snow-covered grass and leisurely watched his owner at work. Jack had taken it upon himself to host the celebrations this year with Charlotte's encouragement, much to the rest of his family's surprise that he would be cooking.

#

London was dusted in white snowflakes as the Christmas tree in the Covent Garden piazza lit up brightly to couples kissing beneath its towering beauty. The smell of rich, mulled wine and roasted chestnuts perfuming the air. Street artists staged their final shows of the year, their waiting hats filled with various shiny coins. It was the time for giving.

#

Carol singers with red noses sweetly recited "Silent Night" as Jack King finished up his outdoor preparations and returned into the warmth, pinching a Christmas chocolate from the tree as he unlaced his boots, toasting his toes by the fire.

The house was peaceful and silent. Jack enjoyed the rare tranquility of his now shared house and took five minutes to reflect on the year. He never intended to, but these moments of solitude were often still filled with thoughts of a certain someone he knew he shouldn't think about anymore.

Jack wanted to wish her a Merry Christmas. Scrolling through the phonebook on his mobile phone with a festive cheer in his heart, he stopped at the letter E. A warm Christmas text message was composed and sent to the number he had saved for Evelyn Wise.

He began to remember the heated moments he and Evelyn shared when he had picked her up for Christmases before. The snow pelting down on the windscreen as the traffic backed up and the glare of red brake lights sent Evelyn's hand reaching up his thigh in the driver's seat. Jack lowered the temperature from the car heaters as his urge to touch Evelyn in return raced through him, his desire taking over.

He remembered how Evelyn would tease the top of his boxers, running her fingers along the Calvin Klein labelled band before reaching inside. Jack, in turn, would fix his free hand firmly on her leg before moving his hand under her laced underwear as he forced himself to focus on the road.

# # #

Charlotte arrived home with the children as Jack returned swiftly from his memories. He checked his phone for Evelyn's reply and deleted the evidence of the message he had sent. He wondered what she would be doing this year and if she would be sharing it with someone special.

Staring back at him blankly was the empty text message mailbox.

She would never reply.

# # #

The Christmas lights were up on every house that owned them. The holiday was a family occasion to revisit treasures stored away in the loft. Mothers stopping their search for illumination to rest on memories, flicking through photo albums of Christmases past.

Smiling faces and Santa hats disguised the heartache that the quietening of this time exposed. In homes around the world many found it difficult to deal with their selves. Time spent in complete solitude during the holidays highlighting unresolved circumstances from the year preceding.

Freshly built snowmen guarded huge houses, their coal coat buttons vertically positioned over bulging stomachs as people all over the world wrapped presents of all shapes and sizes in preparation for the big day. Father Christmas was on his way.

A tantalizing energy danced through the festive season on the morning of Christmas Eve and an unusual package arrived at a red bricked doorstep. The house was filled with the spirit of Christmas. The smell of freshly baked mince pies wafted through the open plan farmhouse kitchen. The pine of the Christmas tree scented the large living room.

Five single, now brown pines had dropped from the tree, settling on unopened presents near the base of the tree as it enjoyed the icy cold water it was submerged in. The bucket the Christmas tree was placed in was covered in traditional Christmas wrapping paper and a big red silk bow.

Smiling gingerbread men dusted in icing sugar were left on the living room table and nibbled at by a middle-aged man who lay enjoying the television. A plastic DVD case from an accompanying box set was perched on the black TV stand, nestled by television remote controls. The sound of the television was momentarily disturbed by the announcement of the final post before Christmas, which rang at the front door.

The postman, a jolly man who embraced the festivities, was wearing a red Santa's hat, complete with a white fluffy band near his forehead. He waited patiently for an answer from the homeowner. Jack King got up from the sofa, his bare feet padding on the newly laid soft cream carpet, rubbing his eyes. Even though it was winter he was wearing shorts, his strong legs visible.

Jack greeted the postman with enthusiasm, complimenting him on his choice of hat. The postman replied that his wife had told his little girls that he was helping out Father Christmas with this year's deliveries and they insisted their dad must wear the correct gear for the important duty.

In addition to a handful of Christmas cards, the late senders had managed to get to him just in time. The postman handed Jack a package. The package was wrapped like a wartime parcel, its wrapping held together with a traditional white piece of string.

Thanking the postman, Jack wandered back inside, the chipper holly and ivy wreath knocking itself against the white front door as he closed it behind him and returned to the warmth of his log fire.

It had been a long time since anyone had delivered dodgy packages to him. Curious, Jack Wise wandered inside, unlacing the white string as he went. It didn't look like a Christmas present, he told himself. The voice of his mother rang in his head as if he were still a child and told not to open presents until tomorrow.

He was yet to identify the contents when Charlotte rang his mobile, her routine lunchtime phone call. It was a constructive attempt to quiet her internal worrying about his whereabouts. She didn't trust him.

Jack was reminded of her Christmas instructions, half of which he had indeed forgotten. She would be home in fifteen minutes she informed him. On Christmas Eve she allowed herself a half day. Leaving the parcel to one side, Jack jumped to his chores.

# # #

Charlotte's Mini Cooper pulled up on the drive. She was happy to be home for Christmas; it had been a tough year for her business. Turning the key in the lock, she called out to Jack who had left a note to say he would be back in five minutes, having popped down to the shops. Unloading the last of her Christmas shopping from the car, Charlotte was pleased to be spending the next week with her family.

She walked towards their newly fitted kitchen and perched herself on a breakfast stall, its leather cushion comforting her. Sitting up at the Ikea kitchen island, Charlotte noticed a parcel that had been half opened. She nosed at it from a bird's eye view, knowing it wasn't addressed to her as she walked towards the kettle. Pouring herself a well earnt cup of tea. Charlotte was unable to resist the temptation any longer and slightly pulled back the crisp, brown paper.

# # #

Pouring in the milk, adding a teaspoon of sugar, she relaxed from the sweeteners as she rested back on the bar stool. With the fresh cup of tea in one hand, her painted nails drummed on the china. The string lay sprawled outside of the parcel, but she was able to reveal the contents inside. Opening it fully she could see a small bag of Cadburys Clusters sat on top of a newly published book embellished by a bound document. The document was laminated. The front page giving the professional paperwork a white exterior which was held together in a black plastic. The black plastic spiral travelled down the left hand edge.

Pushing the treats to one side, Charlotte realised it was a feature film script. Reading the title she became curious. Charlotte paused as her eyes landed on the author and screenwriter's name...Evelyn Wise.

# # #

Chapter 52

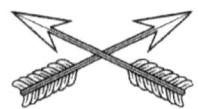

London Love...

The breakdown of roles for a new Twentieth Century Fox feature film arrived in the inboxes of actors' agents around the world. Laptops and computer screens gleamed with the favorable salaries. Commissions were calculated in hopeful anticipation.

The details on the breakdown were much like that of any other recruitment agent. The information detailed the specific requirements the hopeful candidates would need to possess. A slim woman in her late-twenties and a good looking man in his mid-forties would take the leads. Charisma and the ability to compel audiences were a given.

The agents began putting their best actors and actresses forward. Artists were submitted and computer mice clicked away at thumbnail icons of good looking faces with professional urgency.

The casting directors selected their first choices from the submissions and the second stage in the casting process began. Excited actors began rehearsing what they would bring to this particular table.

Two old friends taped in unison from different sides of the transatlantic. Fiddling with the camera, their energy flowing, they uploaded their submissions, their fingers firmly crossed. A frozen yoghurt was enjoyed and an expresso sipped with celebratory energy, concluding their attempts.

Time passed as it usually did after these sorts of things and no word was spoken to neither agent nor artist. The casting director was out of the loop for a week too as the producers and director watched and re-watched the self tapes they had been forwarded.

More breakdowns came and went, flashing up on agent computer screens across the globe. Lunch and coffee breaks offered up a chance to rest computer glared eyes.

The news of the Twentieth Century Fox film was finally parted and two English actors were given the challenge of the lead roles. Their agents called them on their mobiles immediately. The leading lady was based in Los Angeles and had been awoken in the night as she had instructed her English agent to call if fate were to hand her this golden opportunity.

Evelyn Wise danced with happiness out of her bed in America. Life was restored; it was time to live again.

The casting process was in full swing as the director finalized who would play the supporting roles. The feature film scripts were emailed out as the leads and the rest of the cast began their studies of the shoes they would soon fill.

Evelyn Wise read the script, enjoying it from start to finish. She began her study of the leading lady and was overjoyed at finally securing another big break. She smiled to herself proudly. She was a lead in a big budget blockbuster.

# # #

Jack King hadn't been called in for anything in weeks and the silence was frustrating his desire to live out his passion until he checked his inbox later that day. His fate had changed to reveal he had been recast in a feature film lead. He had taped for it before with no luck, but the actor who had been given the role had had a change of personal circumstances.

Charlotte signed the email promising to ring him within the next hour; she was currently on the phone singing Jack's praises to America.

Within a week, the news began to reveal its life changing circumstances, unknowingly Jack and Evelyn had booked their next big breaks and this time, there would be a very familiar face to greet the other on set.

Jack did a celebratory dance in his kitchen, music blaring as he played his favorite track over and over. This was it! Jack checked the internet to see if anyone else's name was attached to the film. Nobody had been listed yet.

As they read and reread their scripts, the accommodation and flights were scheduled by the production team. Further information on the project was kept tight-lipped. Lines were learnt and enough clothes for six weeks of filming were packed.

Each zipped up their belongings in matching North Face suitcases. Their studio sent cars, which waited patiently outside their houses in the darkness of the early hours.

As London Heathrow airport lounge dawned for Jack, Evelyn was a continent away. Jack would be departing for L.A. in less than two hours. Evelyn was already there, now seated in an armchair at her favorite Starbucks on Barrington Court in Brentwood.

Both cradled their new scripts and although neither had learnt about the other being cast, their thoughts were once again in sync.

Both were about to enter the beautiful unknown. They were two actors who shared one ambition and a destiny that would always include the other.

# # #

Coming Soon...
"L.A. Love"

About the author:

Victoria Atkin's writing passion was nurtured as a child when she would write poems and short stories during car journeys with her father. As her academic studies continued, Victoria's flair for writing developed alongside her acting career where she studied at The University of Chichester and The Royal Central School of Speech and Drama.

Victoria has written for The Stage Newspaper and Spotlight, both highly regarded sources of research for the acting communities in the United Kingdom. Her first novel, London Love, will debut in early 2015.

In addition to acting commitments, Victoria continues to develop literature for the world of television and screen including women's romance fiction as well as acting theories and guides.